YOU WON'T BELIEVE THIS

Books by Adam Baron

BOY UNDERWATER

YOU WON'T BELIEVE THIS

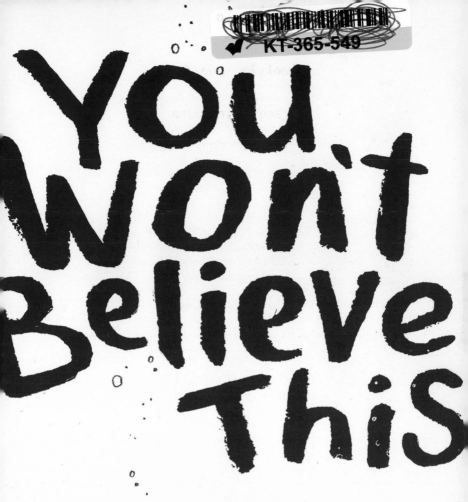

You Won't Believe This

ADAM BARON

HarperCollins *Children's Books*

First published in Great Britain by
HarperCollins *Children's Books* in 2019
HarperCollins *Children's Books* is a division of HarperCollins*Publishers* Ltd,
HarperCollins Publishers
1 London Bridge Street
London SE1 9GF

The HarperCollins website address is:
www.harpercollins.co.uk

1

ISBN 978–0–00–826704–9

Adam Baron and Benji Davies assert the moral right to be identified as the
author and illustrator of the work respectively.

Typeset in Sabon 11/18
Printed and bound in England by CPI Group (UK) Ltd, Croydon CR0 4YY

MIX
Paper from
responsible sources
FSC™ C007454

For Rachel, Frances, Betty and Marjorie – the grandmothers

CHAPTER ONE

Here's something you won't believe.

Veronique Chang did NOT get a Distinction in her Grade 5 piano. In fact, she only just passed! Why should you be surprised? Well. This is Veronique we're talking about – our class genius. Answers LOVE her! They seem to float down to her from the ceiling before they get to anyone else (Marcus Breen calls her Siri). It was her birthday last month and I asked her what she wanted.

'*War and Peace*,' she said, and I frowned at her.

'Greedy.'

'What do you mean?'

'Well, you can't have both,' I said. 'And anyway, I'm not the prime minister, how am I supposed to organise either?'

Veronique looked at me. 'It's a book. By Tolstoy?'

'Oh,' I said. 'Bet it's not as good as *Mr Gum*, though.'

And when I found a copy later in the Blackheath Bookshop I realised that it certainly wasn't.

As for music, Veronique is INCREDIBLE. When she did her Grade 4, Mrs Johnson (our last head teacher) made her stand up in assembly. Veronique, she announced, had got the highest mark in the whole COUNTRY. Veronique wasn't even surprised.

'I was lucky,' she said, looking down at me with a shrug. 'My glissando was off.'

I was about to ask what she meant but Mrs Johnson made her go up to play one of her pieces. Wolfman Amadeus . . . Gocart (I think). And wow! The only time I've seen fingers move as fast was when Lance brought in a bag of Haribos on his birthday.

Marcus Breen started clapping at one point, but that was actually a quiet bit and Veronique went on some more. When she did finish, I stared at her.

'Amazing,' I said. 'If also quite boring.'

Lance agreed. 'You're *brill*iant,' he said. 'Does that mean you can play . . . um . . . ?'

'What?'

He was so in awe he could hardly say it. '*Star Wars*?'

'I don't know,' Veronique answered. 'Who's it by?'

Lance had to think about it. 'Obi-Wan Kenobi.'

'Is he Renaissance or baroque?'

'Jedi,' Lance said.

That was six months ago. She got the Grade 5 back last week. I was at her house. Veronique's mum came into the kitchen waving an envelope. She had a smile on her face – but it faded. Her mum had the envelope in one hand and the results in the other and she just stared at them, amazement about to turn to disbelief, when she sighed – and picked up her phone.

'I think there might have been a mistake,' she said. 'It's Veronique Chang. C. H. A. N. G.'

But there wasn't. The woman on the phone was sure of it. Veronique *hadn't* got a Distinction and she hadn't even got a Merit.

'Well done anyway,' her mum said (because she's really nice). But then she got on the phone again, this time to Veronique's piano teacher, and walked off into the living room to talk to him. I don't think Veronique wanted to be there when she came back so we went outside, then down to the little wooden house at the bottom of their garden where her granny used to live (who she calls Nanai). It was quiet in there. And dusty. We stood for a minute, not speaking, just looking at all the old photographs that lined the walls, and then down at Nanai's chair. It was even emptier than the rest of the place. There was a hollowed-out bit, like the empty spaces we'd seen at the Pompeii exhibition at the British Museum. On top of it was a photograph. Old. Black and white, no glass left in the frame. I picked it up and we both stared at it until Veronique did something that scared me.

She began to cry.

Eeek! I watched her, with no idea WHAT to do until my hand went out, hovering over her shoulder like an X-wing starfighter, just about to land. It stayed there until her dad came in.

'Don't worry, love,' he said, setting a spade down against the wall. 'It's just a grade exam.'

'What?'

'It's okay to be disappointed. But you can do better next time, can't you?'

Veronique didn't answer. Instead she just stared at her dad and shook her head, tears tumbling out of her eyes like kids from a school bus. Then she did something that amazed him. She stopped crying – and began to laugh! She laughed and laughed and didn't stop and her dad was confused. He didn't know why she was laughing, though I did – I knew perfectly well. Of course I did! It was her NOT getting a Distinction! For the first time EVER! It wasn't a *bad* thing. It wasn't something to make her cry.

In fact, believe it or not, getting just a pass on her Grade 5 piano was one of the best things to happen to Veronique Chang in her WHOLE LIFE.

And this book is all about why.

(See you in the next chapter, then.)

TWO-AND-A-HALF WEEKS EARLIER

CHAPTER TWO

It began on a Wednesday. Though not any old Wednesday. A Wednesday when someone did something.

And it was BAD.

And they did it to Mrs Martin.

I am going to repeat that.

They did it to *Mrs Martin*, who is, in my opinion, the best teacher *ever* to exist apart *perhaps* from Socrates, who *our* teacher, Miss Phillips, told us about last week. Socrates was *really* clever and taught this other guy, Plato, in ancient Greece. He's a teacher legend, though Miss Phillips also told us that he drank poison and died, which must really have upset Plato's learning pathway. Plato would *also* have got a supply teacher, wouldn't he, and if *he* was an old horror like Mr Gorton (who we get) Plato would have been IN for it.

It happened after PE. We were up on the heath doing athletics (even though it was *fr-e-e-e-zing*). Mrs Martin does it with us because long before she was an AMAZING teacher she ran for Botswana. She even went to the Olympics, which Lance did too when they were in London (though he was only five). His dad took him but he got so excited he wet himself. By the time they got back from the loos, Usain Bolt had already finished.

'Two hundred pounds,' his dad says, nearly every time I go round. '*Each*, Cymbeline. To see a man jogging round a track with a flag round his shoulders.'

I'd laugh but I can't talk, actually, because when my Uncle Bill took me to the fair once I wet myself on the Ferris wheel. It went down on the man below, who shouted up that he was going to punch Uncle Bill's lights out. When we got off, we had to leg it (as fast as Usain Bolt, actually).

Anyway, our class was up on the heath doing running trials with Mrs Martin to pick who would be on the athletics team. I came third, after Billy Lee and Daisy Blake, though she's so tall I really don't think it's fair. Each one of her legs contains about five of mine. Afterwards, we came back down to school and followed Mrs Martin towards our classroom.

We were just approaching the stairs, and Marcus Breen was doing these incredibly realistic sounds with his armpits (you know what I mean). Mrs Martin wasn't telling Marcus off – she was trying to do *even better ones*. THAT's how cool she is. She was still trying when we all got to the stairs, where she'd left her normal shoes next to one of the drip buckets which catch leaks. Our school's really old and these buckets are dotted about here and there, and now every class has a Drip Monitor who rushes out when it starts raining and makes sure the buckets are in place. There used only to be one or two leaks, but it's been getting worse and there are about ten buckets now.

Anyway, Mrs Martin's shoes were open-top ones, with no straps. We all stopped as she did this little hop thing to get out of her trainers. We watched as she reached out her big toe, using it to slide her right shoe towards her. And it happened, something I need to prepare you for in case you faint, or scream, or simply drop down DEAD when you find out what someone had done.

So here goes—

Brace yourself . . .

I'm going to say it.

No, I really am this time . . .

Actually, I don't think I can say it.

Okay, here goes, really—

They'd put jelly in her shoes.

AND

IT

WAS

BLUE

JELLY.

CHAPTER THREE

Actually, that doesn't sound *too* bad, does it?

Jelly, in her shoes? Even BLUE jelly?

It was almost funny.

The problem was, this was *Mrs Martin*, the most totally superb teacher in the WHOLE world, and *she* didn't seem to see it as funny – and neither did some of the other kids. Vi Delap gasped. Elizabeth Fisher's mouth shot open in amazement, though probably just because she's never done ANYTHING bad in her WHOLE life. Other kids were shocked too – because of WHO this had been done to. You see, it's not just me who thinks Mrs Martin is AMAZING. On our first day in Year 3 she told us all to line up. We were nervous and didn't know what she wanted. Vi was first, all shy and worried, until Mrs Martin grinned at her.

'What's your favourite hobby?' she asked, her voice all soft.

'Football,' Vi said, because she's really good (and no, not just for a girl – sexist!).

Without even *thinking*, Mrs Martin sang:

When you're in goal and the ball flies by,
Who d'you think kicked it? Must be Vi!

Then she did a double high-five with Vi followed by a toe touch and then another toe touch. Vi went bright red and beamed, and then it was Lance's turn. He said cycling, of course (that's his thing), and in a flash Mrs Martin sang:

In front of me is my main man Lance.
He's going to win the Tour de France –
Legally.

She gave Lance a low-five followed by a high-five and then they both pretended they were cycling *really* fast. Lance grinned like a two-year-old in Santa's grotto, and then it was Marcus Breen. He said sleeping, because, well, he's Marcus Breen. We all groaned but Mrs Martin laughed.

Think you're good at snoozing, meet Mr Breen.
This boy's gonna show you how to dream.

She gave Marcus a double cross high-ten and then pretended to sleep. And she did this with *everyone*. EVERY person in our class got their own instant song and their own greeting, though some were harder than others.

'Cymbeline Igloo,' I said.

Mrs Martin drew her hand across her forehead. 'Phew.'

'And I like football but I *also* like art.'

'DOUBLE phew. But here goes.' And she sang:

If you need to get a penalty, don't throw in the towel –
Cymbeline Igloo can draw a foul.

I got a double high fist bump after which I got a double toe touch like Vi, but with Mrs Martin and me both doing air drawing at the same time. And I felt this warmth beginning to grow in the middle of my chest, like there was a radiator in there, until it had reached all the way to my ears. It made me feel special, it made us all feel special – and *every single morning* began like that! This sunny sort of warmth came to us from Mrs Martin and stayed for the whole day. She gave us our own individual greeting with our own rhyme and she NEVER got anyone's wrong. It was amazing, and I can tell you this: nowhere on the *entire* Internet does it say that Socrates did the same thing.

And *he* only had Plato.

So, to see someone play *any* kind of trick on Mrs Martin was probably too much for some of us. Everyone stopped as Mrs Martin gasped and looked down. We all did the same. The jelly (the BLUE jelly) oozed up between her toes like something you might see on *Doctor Who*, though I wouldn't know because my mum says I'm too young to watch it (even if Lance does and he's THREE DAYS younger than me).

Mrs Martin looked confused at first, not quite able to understand what she was seeing. Then her expression changed. And I expected her to be angry. Miss Phillips would have set her face, hands flying out to her hips. Mr Gorton would have gone VESUVIUS.

But what Mrs Martin did was worse somehow.

This brilliant teacher we all love did not frown. Or shout. Or get mad. Instead, she just went still and said, 'Oh . . .', like you might if someone you REALLY like was saying you weren't invited to their birthday party, *and* you'd already bought their present.

And that's when I did something I couldn't quite believe. Mrs Martin stepped back a little. She looked down at us, a sort of not-quite-able-to-believe-it look on her open, worn-in face. Everyone looked away from her, unable to meet her gaze – except for me. When her eyes fell on mine I was suddenly nervous, and unable even to move, because the weirdness of it had crept up on me. Someone putting *jelly* in her shoes? WHAT? It suddenly seemed so bizarre that instead of a radiator in me there were these weird, frothy bubbles.

And I giggled.

I don't know why – honestly! It just came out. A stupid, childish, RIDICULOUS giggle that was SO loud! It stopped Mrs Martin. It stopped me. Mrs Martin looked even more upset – and surprised – and I could see her mind ticking over, and the completely WRONG conclusion about to make itself inside her head.

'No,' I said, as fast as I possibly could. 'That doesn't mean—'

But before I could go on I was interrupted. It was Mr Baker (our new head teacher). He was showing some men round our school, but he turned to Mrs Martin, a curiosity on his face that seemed to snap her away from me. And she turned, bent down and picked up her shoe, along with the other one, which had also been filled with jelly. Then she edged through us all, glancing quickly at me with my face burning, before hurrying off towards the staff room, one hand dangling her shoes, the other held up to her face.

Halfway there she broke into a run.

CHAPTER FOUR

We were quiet that afternoon. We got on with our work. Or tried to. I couldn't: the word IDIOT was trampolining in my brain. At last play I didn't even join in when Billy Lee got his football out, or give my expert opinion on how many goals Jacky Chapman was going to score for Charlton on Saturday. I just looked round the playground as some kids in our class went on as normal while others talked about what had happened.

Lance and Vi Delap were saying how stupid it was, Marcus Breen wondering why anyone would want to waste perfectly good jelly. You should have seen Daisy Blake, though. She LOVES Mrs Martin. When Daisy's grandpa died last year, Mrs Martin was epic, telling her that crying was fine if she wanted to cry, and not if she didn't, changing her morning greeting to add a really long hug at the end, holding Daisy's hand at home time until her mum or dad came. So Daisy was one hundred per cent ANGRY.

'Oh, come on!' I said, when I realised that she was glaring at me. 'I'd never! I wouldn't!'

Daisy studied me, then put her hands on her hips as she turned to look round the playground.

'Then who was it?' she said. 'Who *did* it, Cymbeline?'

And she wasn't the only one who wanted to know that.

Mr Baker held a SPECIAL ASSEMBLY before home time. After we'd all trooped in, he stared down at us from the stage. He went on about respect, and behaviour, and asked for the culprit to come forward. Elizabeth Fisher glanced at me, which made me go bright red again even though I was really trying not to. Did Mrs Martin notice? I kept my head down, hoping she wasn't looking at me.

'Well,' Mr Baker said, when no one owned up. 'I was *told* that this school was full of kind, considerate pupils. And honest ones too. It seems that this might not be true.'

We were all given an envelope which we were told

to take home to our parents. We filed out, my neck and face burning YET AGAIN when I had to walk past Mrs Martin. She was standing next to the wall bars and I could finally sort of understand how Daisy felt. Mrs Martin was trying to look cheerful, as if it was all just some stupid thing.

But she couldn't really manage it.

I kept my head down and followed Vi into the playground, where Daisy was sucking on a new stick of rock (which she must have snuck into her schoolbag because there was NO WAY her parents could have allowed her to bring it in). She was glaring at the passing kids.

'What are you looking at?' said Billy Lee, when it was his turn.

'You tell me,' said Daisy, pointing the stick of rock at him. I thought they might get into an argument actually, but his mum was there to pick him up so he walked off.

There was no one there to pick me up – not yet anyway. I do ICT club after school on Wednesdays because Mum works. I'd rather do football but that costs more and, anyway, Mum says I can use the time to catch up on my homework.

'Spellings especially,' she says.

I want to argue – but I can't really. Spellings! There are just so many letters! And the way they join together, the Is and Es always swapping places like Year 1 kids trying to wind up Mrs Mason. We've also started doing these things called apostrophes, which at first I didn't understand.

'They show you *own* something,' Miss Phillips said. 'Like "Cymbeline's football".'

I nodded but I still didn't get it. Everyone knows that it's Billy's football. As for where you put the apostrophes in the actual words, that's just not possible to know. You may as well be playing pin the tail on the donkey. I can't wait until I can use a computer to do my writing because of the wavy red lines that help you out, and it makes me wonder: why has no one invented a pencil which does that?

'Hi, Cym,' Mum said later that day, putting her head round the door of the ICT suite. 'Ready?'

I said I was and when she'd signed me out I put my coat on. I followed her into the playground and through the gate on to the road. There were some men out there with clipboards, staring at the school and making notes. One was even on the roof. The police . . . ? Mr Baker really was taking this jelly thing seriously. I grabbed Mum's hand and pulled her up the steps towards Blackheath.

Now, if I've done something at school which perhaps I shouldn't have, I would NOT normally want to tell my mum. This time, though, I did want to tell her, because Mum *knows* Mrs Martin. They're both in the Friends' Forum, which raises money for St Saviour's. They do things like getting everyone to bake cakes to sell to themselves at the school fair and they ask parents to donate back the same bottles of cheap wine they won at the last fair and didn't drink. Toys as well. In Year 2, Lance's mum donated his old Buzz Lightyear for the Christmas Fair without telling him. Darren Cross won it in the tombola. Neither of them knew until Darren's mum donated it *back* for the Easter Fair without telling *him*, and who should pull it out of the lucky dip? Lance!

'Buzz!' he exclaimed. 'I thought you'd gone back to Gamma 4!'

When his mum saw it at home later, she said she thought she was going crazy.

The reason I wanted to tell Mum was simple – I had to explain my giggle. I wanted her to tell Mrs

Martin that it was *just* a giggle and that I DID NOT PUT JELLY IN HER SHOES. The idea that she might think it was me was terrible, not least because she'd have to tell Mr Baker, wouldn't she? So I started to tell Mum – but she wasn't listening. First she had to find her car keys, which always takes ages because her bag's like the TARDIS (well, probably – ask Lance, why don't you?). Then, when we were finally in the car, she just said things like 'Oh dear' and 'What a shame', before coming out with something totally and utterly RANDOM.

'Cym,' she said, putting her hand on my arm, 'you do want me to be happy, don't you?'

Now *that* was a weird question, and not only because it had nothing at ALL to do with Mrs Martin (or jelly). Before Christmas, Mum had been totally *not* happy, and that had been horrible. Had she asked me *then* if I wanted her to be happy, I'd have said yes, of course – but she seemed happy enough *now*. And why wouldn't she be – Charlton were up to third! Also, my last school report was, and I quote, 'not quite as bad as the last one'.

She'd also got a new job teaching art, which meant we could afford a car now, and she'd started going out to the cinema on Friday nights with this new friend of hers called Stephan.

'You mean even happier?' I asked.

'Maybe.'

'Like in *The Sound of Music*?'

'Why not?'

'We'd better hope Charlton beat Wigan, then. Though no singing in front of my friends. Why are you asking?'

Mum went red. 'Something happened today.'

'What?'

'Just . . . something I need to think about.'

'But it's a good thing?'

'I hope so. But I have to think first. Actually, forget I said anything, okay?'

Mum put the key in and I shrugged, happy to forget it because I *wanted to go back to the subject of Mrs Martin*. Even now, my favourite teacher could be asking herself what she'd done to turn me against her. When I got back to telling Mum, though, she got distracted *again*. I was just getting to the bit where we came down from the heath, when Mum's phone rang.

'Hello?' she said, sounding a little surprised by who was calling. I tried to carry on talking, but Mum put her hand up. Her face went serious and she said, 'Of course,' and 'Right away,' before hanging up. She started the car, did a three-point turn, and thirty seconds later we were shooting across the little roundabout as I asked her what was going on.

'Is it Mrs Martin?' I said, my voice a bit wobbly. 'Does she want to see you?'

The answer was no, because Mrs Martin lives in Westcombe Park, and three minutes later we were pulling up outside a house on the other side of Blackheath Village.

Veronique's house.

And in the driveway was an ambulance.

CHAPTER FIVE

The first time I met Veronique's granny she was asleep in her chair. Veronique took me down to her little wooden house. We'd brought her tea, but instead of watching her drink it I looked at all the photos on the wall showing her with Veronique when Veronique was little, and even older ones when she herself had been a child, standing with her mum, dad and sister with some boats behind them.

I would have liked to ask her about that time, and just talk to her generally, because I don't have any grandparents, and people say they're fun. Apparently they give you sweets and pound coins AND they fall asleep when you're watching telly (which means you don't have to stop). Veronique's granny didn't do any of these things that first time I saw her because she didn't wake up, making me wonder what the point of her was.

But the next time was different.

'So,' she said, squinting at me through these MASSIVE glasses. '*You're* the famous Cymbeline. What sort of a name is that, might I ask?'

'Nanai!' Veronique said.

'I don't mind. It's Shakespeare, Veronique's granny.'

'I know that! I'm not completely gaga, you know. And call me Nanai. But Shakespeare used normal names as well, didn't he? Duncan, Richard, Henry . . .'

'But I could have been called Hamlet,' I said. 'Or Romeo.'

'Well, let's agree that it could have been worse, then.' Nanai crossed her feet over on this little footstool she had. 'But what have you got to say for yourself, young man?'

It was a surprising question and I didn't know how to answer it at first. But I talked about Saturday football, which we do on the heath, and then Charlton, and how I hoped they'd be up in the Premier League by the time I started playing for them.

'You want to be a footballer, then?'

'Of course. Jacky Chapman's even got his own

helicopter! He's got a pilot's licence and he flies himself around.'

'Jacky . . . ?'

'*Chapman*. He's the captain. I'm doing my Person Project on him.'

'Your . . . ?'

'You have to find out about someone amazing,' interrupted Veronique. (She does that. I mean, a lot.) 'And do a presentation. I'm doing a scientist.'

'Einstein?'

'No. Niels Bohr.'

'Niels Boring,' I said. 'Jacky Chapman's going to fly me to a match *and* he's going to fly me home.'

'*Is* he?'

'Well, I've written to him. I asked if he'd fly his helicopter to school and pick me up. Haven't heard back yet.'

'Seems you really like football, Cymbeline.'

'Course. Did you ever play?'

Nanai said no, and when I told her how Daisy and Vi, and Vi's sister Frieda, were all really good, she pushed herself up from her chair. I fetched the ball I'd given Veronique for Christmas (which looked *suspiciously clean*) and we played in their garden. Nanai hopped about like *crazy*. Defensively she was very strong (her walking stick helped). As an attacking midfielder she was also impressive. She might not have got round Jacky Chapman, but she nutmegged Veronique no bother and scored a goal between two flowerpots. She was tired then, so I only added two minutes on for stoppages. We helped her back to her chair and she beamed at both of us. Veronique especially.

Veronique sat on the edge of her chair and Nanai took her hand before doing something a bit weird. She pushed Veronique's index finger into a triangle and gave it a little nibble! Veronique rolled her eyes.

'She says it's because I'm so delicious,' she explained. 'When I was a baby she wanted to eat me.'

Nanai giggled, and Veronique rolled her eyes again (though I could tell she secretly loved it). And then Veronique brought Nanai up to date on her French and Chinese classes, fencing competitions, violin, clarinet, ukulele and piano lessons, and how she'd recently got into Tolstoy.

'At your age! Do *you* like Tolstoy, Cymbeline?'

'I like *Toy Story*. Lance has got a Buzz Lightyear.'

'Your brother, is he, this Lance?'

'Friend. I don't have a brother – or a sister,' I added,

which seemed to be a mistake because Nanai stared at me before getting a little panicked, until she turned to the photos on the table by her chair. There was one of a big ship, another of people who looked like they were probably her parents. She grabbed the third one, though – just her as a young woman with another young woman who looked just like her.

Nanai clung to the picture, tight, mumbling to herself as she drifted off to sleep.

Veronique reached forward and pulled Nanai's rug up over her knees. 'She holds on to it all night,' she said, meaning the photograph.

'What? Why?'

'It's a photo of her and Thu,' said Veronique.

'Thu?'

'Her twin sister. You know I told you Nanai was a refugee?'

I did know. It was one of the things that made Veronique and her family SO interesting. Nanai had been one of what British people called the Vietnamese boat people – refugees, like the people fleeing horrible things now are. They were Hoa, Chinese people living in Vietnam, and they had to escape from Vietnam because the government was burning their houses.

'Well, their ship sank,' said Veronique. 'Or something like that. I'm not *too* sure. Nanai was rescued. Her sister wasn't.'

Oh NO.

I looked down at Nanai, that second time I met her, and felt like such an IDIOT. Talking about not having a sister! I couldn't believe I'd done it.

'Not your fault,' said Veronique, guessing what I was thinking. 'Come on.'

She pulled me into the garden.

'I should have told you,' she said, 'about Thu. It's why Nanai hates being asked about being a refugee. She won't talk about it.'

'Blimey. And they were twins? Were they identical?'

'No. Nanai was a tomboy, she says.'

'You can tell that by the football.'

'But Thu was quiet and arty. Musical. And really

beautiful. Nanai says that's where I . . .'

'What?'

Veronique blushed. 'Doesn't matter. Anyway, I wish I had a sister, don't you?'

I blinked at Veronique, not knowing how to answer. For some reason I thought about Stephan's two little girls, who he brings over at the weekend sometimes. They're okay and the little one's cute, actually. She climbs on my knee and calls me Thimbeline. She draws pictures of me that are hilarious.

But I just shrugged.

I couldn't get the image out of my head, of Nanai clutching that photo like it was a swimming float. Something to keep her safe.

It made me feel close to her and for a second I didn't know why. But then I did. You see, I've lost someone too. It happened when I was tiny, though, and I never knew them. I couldn't imagine what it must have been like for Nanai to lose her twin the way she did.

I shivered, and then Veronique's dad called us in for supper. All through it I thought of that photo in Nanai's hands, and how frail and tired she looked as she clung on to it.

CHAPTER SIX

So when Mum drove me round after school and I saw the ambulance in the driveway I was really scared – for Nanai.

And, sure enough, when Mum and I walked into their kitchen, Veronique's dad told us that Nanai was 'having a little trouble with her breathing'.

I swallowed. 'What kind of trouble?'

'They're not sure, Cymbeline,' he said, trying too hard to sound cheerful. 'They're taking her into hospital. Just a precaution,' he added, putting his hand on Veronique's shoulder. 'The medics are just having a little look at her before they go.'

'Can I go down and see her?'

Veronique's dad said better not, which was a shame.

He was going to go with her to the hospital and Veronique's mum was away playing music concerts, so Veronique was coming home with us.

'For a sleepover?'

'Yes,' Mum said. 'And she's very welcome, isn't she, Cymbeline?'

Welcome? A sleepover – ON A WEDNESDAY? And with Veronique, who I used to like so much I couldn't even talk to her?

'Suppose,' I said.

'Can I bring Kit-Kat?'

'PLEASE!' I bellowed, knowing I shouldn't be too excited, because Nanai was ill. But I couldn't help it.

'Course,' Mum said, 'though I think we've got some Mars bars at home somewhere, so . . .'

Mum didn't get to finish because Veronique ran off up the stairs, while we went out to the car with the bag her dad had packed for her.

Mum got in the car while I climbed in the back. Mum and Mr Chang chatted quietly through the window until Veronique came out. She was carrying a big plastic box, covered in a cloth, which she set on the seat between us. Mum was already getting the car started so she didn't see it – not until we got back to our house. We parked opposite and Veronique lifted the box out.

'Oh . . .' Mum said, 'Kit-Kat. Silly of me. I thought you meant . . . But what *is* that?'

'He's a—'

'HAMSTER!' I shouted, as we started to cross the road.

'How sweet,' Mum said, and then spent five minutes hunting in her bag for the house keys.

Now, what I'd just done is BAD, and I certainly don't want you to think that fibbing to my mum is something I do *very* often. I was only trying to protect her, though, because Mum is afraid of EVERYTHING. Daddy-long-legs make her scream like that kid in *Home Alone*. If a wasp flies in the kitchen window, she makes me hide under the table with her until it's gone. She asked Uncle Bill round for lunch last Sunday and I swear it was only because she'd seen a spider on the bathroom ceiling the night before. When he arrived, she shoved the sweeping brush in his hand and pushed him up the stairs.

'And hurry up!' she shouted. 'I really need a wee!'

So, I did fib, but fibbing about Kit-Kat's true

41

identity was not as bad as you might think. Because he is not, as I told Mum, a hamster.

He's a RAT.

And he is *epic*.

Kit-Kat can shake hands with you. He can fetch things. He loves the piano, climbing up on to Veronique's shoulder whenever she practises. He's a great tightrope walker, and can do the high jump, put a ring on your finger, recognise people, and even untie your shoelaces! He can't tie them yet (but Lance can barely do that) and Veronique's training him – and I know who I'd bet on to get there first. Veronique's trained Kit-Kat a lot in fact, but he was like that even before, because Veronique's dad's a scientist and Kit-Kat came from his lab. He is in fact the Veronique of the rat world.

I have another confession too. Kit-Kat being there made me forget about Mrs Martin. I'd planned on spending the whole night thinking about what had happened, but once we were in the house I pulled Veronique up the stairs.

'Supper in an hour,' Mum said. 'What would you like to do, Veronique?'

'Don't worry, Mum, we're going to play Subbuteo.'

Mum wondered whether that was something Veronique would *really* like to do, but I didn't listen. I dragged Veronique up to my room and pulled the Subbuteo box out from under my bed.

Now Subbuteo, which is a game with little plastic footballers that you flick at a ball, is excellent normally, and I knew Veronique would have enjoyed it – but teaching Kit-Kat to play was going to be even better! And, as expected, he was ACE. His dribbling was as good as Mo Salah's and somehow he knew to stay on the pitch (though he trod on the players' heads until I gave him a yellow card). Soon he was taking the ball *round* the players instead of over them and then slipping it past the keeper, all for the reward of a dried pea, which Veronique had brought and which he's obsessed with. It was great, but at 5–0 to Kit-Kat I put the pitch away. Mum had been right: Veronique didn't seem to be into it. I turned to her.

'Is it Mrs Martin? That was totally weird, wasn't it? But *you* shouldn't be upset about it. No one thinks it was you, do they?'

'It isn't that,' Veronique said.

I slapped my forehead. I'd got carried away with the Subbuteo – it was Nanai of course.

'But it's just a precaution,' I said. 'Your dad did say that, didn't he?'

Veronique looked down at her lap. 'Yes, but . . .'

'What?'

'He's an adult.'

'So?'

'You can't believe them when they talk about things like this.'

'*Can't* you?'

'No,' Veronique said, and I realised that she was right. There are pointless things that adults insist you DO know about (apostrophes, hello?) and then some really important stuff they keep from you, like news stories that make them dive forward and turn off the radio. Nanai was as bad. She refused to tell Veronique much about being on the boat from Vietnam. All Veronique knew was that Nanai's family had been part of the Chinese Hoa people in Vietnam. When they had to leave Vietnam by boat, some of them ended up here. There had to be more to know than that, though. And now – was her dad doing the same thing? Was Nanai really ill?

I swallowed. I had an empty feeling in my stomach until I heard Mum climbing up the stairs. I got Kit-Kat back in his box in time but Mum still crouched down to him.

'Let's have a look, then,' she said.

'Sorry. It's his bedtime.'

Mum frowned. 'I thought gerbils slept in the daytime.'

'Oh,' said Veronique, 'he's not a gerbil. He's a—'

'HAMSTER!' I shouted. 'But he's tired now, so . . .'

'Oh, come on,' Mum insisted. 'Just a little peek.' And I couldn't stop her. She lifted the lid and I got my hands near my ears ready for the scream, shuffling aside so I didn't get trampled on when Mum ran to the door. Fortunately, though, Kit-Kat was tucked up in his straw with just his little face poking out.

'Sweet!' Mum said as Kit-Kat gave her a nose twitch. And we went downstairs for supper.

Mum had made bacony pasta. I love it, and Veronique said she did too, though she didn't eat much. If I left mine, Mum would have made me finish it, but she just smiled at Veronique and squeezed her elbow. Back upstairs we took it in turns getting ready for bed and when Veronique came out of the bathroom I blinked. I'd never seen her in pyjamas. These were Chinese ones that folded over in the middle. She looked really different and it made me think of the photos of Nanai, how she'd been rescued, how she'd come from another place, somewhere Veronique was linked to, though she's so part of our school and Blackheath. It made me wonder if anyone in my past had run away from somewhere, though I didn't get long to think about it. Veronique was pale. She was quiet as we blew her bed up, *and* through part of Narnia, which Mum read us. I don't think it was because of the White Witch either because she was still like that as she climbed into her sleeping bag.

Mum kissed me goodnight and gave Veronique a hug. She put the light out and when we were on our own I stared down at Veronique through the faint blue glow from my ghostie light.

'Is it still Nanai? Is that why you're upset?'

Veronique didn't answer.

I remembered what Mr Prentice said, the art therapy man I went to after Mum got ill before Christmas. You have to let it out. The thing you're scared of. So I said, 'Did something happen? Before the ambulance came, I mean?'

There was silence again but somehow I knew the answer was yes.

'Did Nanai fall over?'

'No.'

'Or be sick?'

'No,' Veronique said, again.

'Then what? *What?*'

'I went down to see her. Earlier.'

'To play football?'

'Just see her.'

'And?'

'She was sitting there, in her chair. She didn't even . . .'

'What?'

'She didn't even want to nibble my finger. She just

47

looked weird. So I asked her what the matter was.'

'And?'

'She told me not to worry.'

'Well, then. Phew.'

'She was really definite about that. It was all very normal, she said. And natural.'

'What was?'

Veronique was about to answer but she hesitated, fiddling with the sleeve of her pyjamas. I looked down at her but she wouldn't look at me, just lay there in the faint blue light. There was silence until Mum started banging pots around in the kitchen, after which the silence came back again. It grew bigger, sort of heavy, and dark-seeming, so that for a second it was like everything in the whole world had stopped.

'*What* was?' I insisted, and Veronique stopped fiddling with her sleeve.

'She said she was going to die, Cymbeline.'

CHAPTER SEVEN

I had bad dreams. They seemed to last all night, though when I woke up they ran off like kids playing Grandmother's Footsteps. Their place was taken by Veronique and I blinked at her. She was kneeling by my bed. With her face washed. And she was dressed. She even had her hair tied up.

'Where's your piano?' she asked.

I groaned and pulled the duvet over my head. 'You can't miss it. It's next to the Ferrari.'

'Where's that, then?'

'It was a joke,' I said, which made Veronique sigh because jokes are the ONE thing she's not good at. They're like apostrophes are to me. Marcus Breen is always getting her. We were in the lunch queue on

Friday and he poked her in the ribs.

'Look under there,' he told her. Veronique frowned.

'Under where?'

'There!'

'Under *where*?' Veronique asked again, and Marcus sniggered.

'You said "underwear"!' he said.

'I know, and you won't tell me. Under WHERE?'

Marcus really burst it and Veronique asked why he was laughing.

'No reason. What does a dog do when it's hot?'

'Pants.'

Marcus nearly went blue. I thought he was going to choke to death. When he'd recovered, he said that a teacher has five boys in her class, all named Will.

'To tell them apart she calls the first one Will A, the second one Will B, and so on. So what's the fifth one called?'

Veronique was about to answer, but luckily we got to the front of the queue and Mrs Stebbings dolloped out the curry.

Anyway, when I explained that we didn't *have* a piano, Veronique stared like I'd said we didn't have a sofa.

'But my exam's a week on Saturday! I didn't get to practise last night because of Nanai. And I always practise on Thursday *mornings* because it's fencing after school so I can't play *tonight*. Or I can, but I'll stay up late so I won't be able to get up early the *next* morning. And that means—'

'Calm down,' I said, shoving the duvet aside and reaching for the art box.

After what Veronique had told me last night, I wanted to do all I could for her. I was upset about Nanai myself but she wasn't *my* grandmother, was she? It was bound to be worse for Veronique and I couldn't imagine what she must be feeling. So, downstairs, I got some sheets of paper and Sellotaped them to the kitchen table. Veronique told me where the keys all went and I drew a piano. Veronique said there should be pedal things underneath, so I got my wellies. She told me she was going to play a piece called the 'Four Seasons', which I was excited about – but it turned out it had nothing to do with pizza. It was still good, though – better than her piece in assembly, actually, because it was quiet and I could listen to it *and* Harry Potter on Mum's phone at the same time. I recommend this kind of piano and would like to suggest to all classical musicians that they think a bit more about the people who may have to be sitting close to them when they're playing.

I hoped that getting to practise would cheer Veronique up. But it didn't, much, so I had another idea – I gave her the phone to call her dad.

'So?' I asked, after she'd hung up.

'The doctors can't find anything wrong with her.'

'Brilliant!'

'I suppose.'

'What do you mean? Nanai's not a doctor, is she? They're bound to know better than her, aren't they?'

'I suppose,' said Veronique again, and then Mum appeared, her eyes going wide as Frisbees to see me standing there.

The reason for Mum's reaction was that I am normally just a *tiny* bit reluctant to get out of bed in the morning. Schooldays especially. Mum says it was the same when I was being born, only getting me out of bed is even more painful than getting me out of *her*.

'Gas and air!' she shouts, yanking at my duvet. 'Get me the gas and air!'

It's not my fault, though. It's bed. At night you complain about having to get into it, but – magically – by the morning it's become this perfect thing you don't want to get out of. A quick splash of the face followed by a bowl of Weetabix are NOTHING compared to it.

'Veronique,' Mum said, 'can you come over every night?'

I soon wished the same thing, because it wasn't Weetabix for breakfast that morning like I normally have: Mum made scrambled eggs. On a Thursday! Then Veronique fed Kit-Kat and, because we hadn't really thought what we'd do with him that day, Mum called Veronique's dad and asked him to take Kit-Kat back to their house again.

He met us at the top of the school steps and told us again about Nanai. They'd done this test and that test, but they couldn't find *anything* wrong.

'That's great,' Mum said. 'Such a relief. Though Veronique's welcome any time. With Kit-Kat of course. What a sweet hamster.'

'Oh, he's not a hamster,' Veronique's dad said with a frown. 'He's a—'

'GERBIL!' I shouted.

'Really?' Mum said. 'I could have sworn you said . . . Anyway, he's adorable.'

'And very good at Subbuteo,' I added.

CHAPTER EIGHT

Now, after what happened yesterday, I'm sure you were expecting me to have been VERY nervous about going into school. And I was – to start with. But then I saw the van, which I'd completely forgotten about.

It was big and red and right outside the gates.

'Yes!' I said, and even Veronique hurried up when she saw it.

We joined the kids crowding round the van, until Miss Phillips shooed us towards the door where Frieda Delap, in Reception, was standing with this big medal round her neck. She was the one we had to thank. She'd been to the Science Museum before Christmas with her family – and seen a competition. You had to write a science-based story right there and then, which your mum or dad typed into a screen. She entered her story and a month later Mrs Johnson (our last head teacher) read it out in assembly.

And it was hilarious. A creature called a Pigglyboo saved the world from climate change by replacing coal and gas with energy from people's lost odd socks. Veronique objected that *that* wasn't very scientific but no one else cared: Frieda won! And she got not only loads of science books and posters for our classrooms but some science experiments here in our OWN SCHOOL!

'I still don't think the sock supply would be reliable,' grumbled Veronique as we walked into the hall.

'It would in our house,' said Mrs Martin. 'We've got thousands of them.'

It stopped me in my tracks to see Mrs Martin, but then I was SO relieved. She smiled at me with her big, gappy-toothed face – JUST LIKE SHE NORMALLY DID.

Pheeeeeeeeeeeeeeeeeeeeeeeeeeeewwwwwwwwww.

Panic over.

Five minutes later, after calming down the BUZZING hall, Mr Baker told us what was going to happen. Each class was getting its *own* genuine Science

Museum scientist – for the WHOLE day. We'd do experiments in our classroom before we all met up later for a finale. I was psyched, and then even more so when we got back to our class. I'd been expecting a wacky old man with fuzzy hair, but instead we got Jen, who had tattoos up her arms and hair that wasn't fuzzy but short – and bright pink.

'Okay, everyone,' she said, 'sit down.'

We did that, and Daisy put her hand up. 'What are we going to do?' she asked.

Jen studied us. 'I'm going to show you something that you've clearly never seen before.'

'What?'

'Soap,' Jen said.

Now, at first, I was a *bit* disappointed: what could be fun about *soap*? It certainly *isn't* fun in our house. Mum makes me use it, which I can mostly understand, though not when she insists on me washing underneath some places and behind others WHICH NO ONE IS GOING TO SEE.

But Jen showed us that soap *could* be fun. First we made soap-powered boats and raced them in trays. Mine came third, after Billy Lee's and Daisy Blake's. (How weird is that?) Next we put washing-up liquid and food dye into milk and made these incredible patterns. Then we made bubbles that filled the whole classroom. We chased those, before making some that were so big we got to go inside them, peering out through the weird colours. It was SO great and, let me tell you, it is *such* a waste of soap that we use it to wash with.

That took us to lunch. After eating I discussed the Wigan game with Mrs Stebbings, our head dinner lady, who is even madder about Charlton than I am. Get this – her sister knows Jacky Chapman's dad's brother's postman's daughter! Outside I stood with the others, wondering what we were going to do later, watching the scientists setting up the last experiment of the day on the AstroTurf.

Back in class we started to learn about forces, Jen explaining what made the soap boats move. I asked about helicopters because of Jacky Chapman having his own and she told me all about this thing called 'lift'. Then we made more boats using other things for power, like birthday candles and rubber bands, and then Jen put some cups and plates from the canteen on a tablecloth. I thought she was going to have her lunch, but as fast as she could she pulled the cloth off, leaving all the cups right there on the table!

'I am *so* trying that at home,' said Marcus Breen.

That took us up to two o'clock. We did a demonstration of our boats to the other kids and then went into their classes to see what they'd been doing. Year 3 had made rockets with balloons. I liked that, but what I was really interested in was Mrs Martin. But again she treated me normally and seemed normal herself. Double phew. After that we went into Year 2, where they'd balanced huge weights on eggs. Year 5 was next. They'd turned their whole classroom into a space station, which was wicked – but you should have SEEN the Year 6 thing.

They'd been working in the hall. After seeing all the other classes, everyone trooped in there. We sat down and looked at Mr Ashe (their teacher). He was sitting on a chair, which was on this circle of wood with red canisters on either side. No one had any idea what it was until the Year 6 scientist stepped forward and pressed a button.

And Mr Ashe lifted off.

A hovercraft! They'd made a real hovercraft! Mr Ashe shot across the hall, spinning round and round, and was about to crash into us when the scientist grabbed him. He spun a few times more and then all the Year 6 kids had a go. Some just lifted off a bit, squealing in excitement and fright before letting themselves down. But Vi and Frieda's brother Franklin went mad, knocking over two drip buckets and nearly whacking into Mrs Martin, who only escaped by leaping up the wall bars. She wasn't cross, though. She was really laughing, which made me feel even more relieved.

I looked around at all the kids, whooping and screaming with Mrs Martin, when Franklin whizzed to the other side of the hall. And I asked myself, did it *really* happen? Did someone *really* play that trick on her? Everyone looked so happy that I couldn't believe it. Or if they had then they hadn't meant anything bad by it. Or – DOH – they couldn't have known they were *Mrs Martin*'s shoes! They just saw random shoes.

That was it, of course!

But it wasn't long before I realised that I was

WRONG.

BECAUSE

THE JELLY

IN THE

SHOES

WAS

NOTHING

COMPARED

TO WHAT

HAPPENED

NEXT.

CHAPTER NINE

If the hovercraft had been the last thing we saw, the day would have been excellent. But once all the Year 6es had had a go we went out to the playground. In front of us was a table. It was covered now with a sheet, though at lunchtime we'd seen what was underneath – a thick plastic chimney with a rocket peeking out. On top was a toy frog called Phil, who was, as Jen now explained, going to fly up to the stars.

'And he's really nervous, so can we all give a cheer to encourage him?'

After the yelling had died down, the teachers told us to sit on the AstroTurf. Jen told us all about the chemicals in the bucket that were going to cause the explosion that would launch the rocket, though if you want to know what they were you'd better ask Veronique – the rest of us were arguing about how high Phil the frog would go. Up to the side wall? The back wall? As high as the heath? Maybe we'd lose sight of him and Major Tim Peake would be blinking in amazement to see a stuffed frog go flying past his window. We were still arguing when Jen asked us all for a countdown.

'TEN!'

The scientists put plastic glasses on and stood next to the table, facing us.

'NINE!'

The teachers stepped to the side and the Reception kids at the front squeezed back.

'EIGHT!'

Jen moved to the side of the playground, where she picked up a little blowtorch and turned it on.

'SEVEN!'

She knelt down and pointed the flame at some powder piled up on a metal tray.

'SIX!'

The powder lit up, fizzing and crackling until, like a red mouse, it began to scurry along an open metal pipe towards the table.

'FIVE!'

When the red mouse was nearly at the table, Jen leapt up, ran towards the table and grabbed hold of the sheet.

'FOUR!'

The mouse flame climbed up the pipe, spluttering for a second then stopping and making us all think it would go out.

'THREE!'

It managed to stay lit, though, going up again as Jen pulled off the sheet to reveal Phil the frog, on his rocket, just about to head up to the . . .

No—

Not Phil.

Not Phil at all.

WHERE WAS PHIL?

We all stared. The scientists, including Jen, were all looking at *us* – they weren't looking behind them at the table. And it was weird, *really* weird, because Phil the frog certainly wasn't there. Someone must have taken him off. The rocket *was* there, and something ELSE was on it.

'TWO!'

That was the scientists. They'd shouted it, not us, or not many of us, just a few of the smaller kids. Because we were staring, hardly able to believe what we were seeing, the scientists looking confused too – by our reaction – until one by one they turned their heads, to see what we were looking at. And what we were looking at was their experiment – the bucket, the rocket, and the thing tied to it – though instead of what they thought was tied to it there was something else.

Not a frog.

A bag.

A blue, rectangular sports bag, pretty old, with a black stripe across the middle, a bag that was familiar to every single person in our school because of what was on the side of it. Five rings. In different colours. Three on top and two below.

Olympic rings, all linked together with a date above and a word underneath in bold.

BOTSWANA.

Everyone stared. And then everyone's head swivelled left to where Mrs Martin was standing, her hands still held up in little fists with what had been excitement but which had now been replaced by shock. And surprise. And disbelief. She shook herself together and looked around, at her feet, as if to find her bag there, as if it couldn't possibly be where it actually *was* – ON TOP OF THAT ROCKET.

There wasn't a 'ONE!' We just watched, no one able to move as the snapping red flame reached the bottom of the bucket. And it shook, with a really loud **BANG.** And the rocket took off, though it didn't go as far as we'd expected. Not to the side wall. Not up to the heath. Just half a metre, before it nosedived on to the table where it rested, as Mrs Martin's bag slid down on to the ground.

Silence. It struck the teachers and the scientists and all of us sitting on the AstroTurf. No one said a word. Not even Marcus Breen. We all just watched as the bag Mrs Martin had got at the Olympics fizzled and gurgled and spluttered.

And

then

it

CHAPTER TEN

I think I need to tell you a bit more about Mrs Martin. She's got this gappy smile, like I've said, that is impossible not to smile back at. You can hear her laugh ALL around the school. She teaches Year 3 but does dance routines at lunchtimes with the Year 5 and 6 girls (but only if they play ABBA songs). She begs you not to tell Mr Martin about her mid-morning Twix or how she really wishes she'd married someone called Mr Kipling instead of him. She cheers all the teams on at Saturday football.

She works on the Friends' Forum, like I said, but I didn't tell you she was in charge of it, sending out all the letters and emails and organising the fairs and coffee mornings and cake sales and sponsored walks and the carol singing round Blackheath every year. I didn't tell you that she stays late to clear up after all the evening events because the parents have to get their kids to bed (hers are grown up).

And I didn't tell you something I learned from Mum, about when all the windows were being replaced in our school. Mrs Martin was the one who found out that the builders were putting in cheaper ones than the ones they'd promised, which wouldn't have been so soundproof. She forced the council to get them done properly, which means we can all learn in peace. The most important thing, though, is how she makes us feel: good, and safe. Like we're at home and not at school. Absolutely everyone has called her Mum by mistake at some point – SO embarrassing – and when she tells you that you can do something, you believe her. You can't help it – and then it turns out to be true.

We have four different houses in our school. They're named after inspiring people like Nelson and Rosa Parks (which I'm in). When I was on the school council I started a petition to get one of the houses renamed and I'm sure you can guess whose name I wanted. Yes – Jacky Chapman, the best captain Charlton have ever had. I'm still waiting to hear about that, but if they say no I'll definitely suggest Mrs Martin instead because she's AMAZING.

So how could anyone DO that to her?

CHAPTER ELEVEN

Auntie Mill picked me up that day. Her and Mum, which was weird. Why were they *both* there? I didn't really think about it, though, because the Mrs Martin thing was too huge.

Jelly – so what? But THIS . . . ?

As I climbed into Auntie Mill's car I kept seeing Mrs Martin's bag before it was blown up, and then again twenty seconds later, after Jen had put it out with a fire extinguisher. It was all blackened and melted, with a gaping hole in the side. And I saw Mrs Martin walking forward and picking it up off the ground, staring at it in total shock before using the same expression as she turned around.

And stared at US.

We'd all stared back, in SILENCE, until Mr Baker towered over us.

'Classrooms!'

We'd marched off and I felt SO terrible that I got this feeling you might recognise from your own school, when someone's done something bad. It really did feel like it was me who'd actually done it. And when I passed Mrs Martin it got worse. I didn't giggle. Not this time. But instead my face went red. And Mrs Martin had been looking at me. I didn't actually see her because I was keeping my eyes on Daisy right ahead of me, but I could FEEL it, her eyes following me all the way into school and up the stairs, the tops of my ears prickling with heat when I got there.

'Had a good day?' Mum asked as Auntie Mill pulled away, barging in front of Lance's mum's Fiesta. I didn't say anything. I just wanted to get home so I could talk to her on her own about what had happened.

AND GET HER TO CALL MRS MARTIN.

But again I didn't get a chance to.

I expected Auntie Mill to turn right at the little roundabout – towards our house. Instead she went up through Blackheath to *her* house, which is next door to Veronique's, actually (Billy Lee lives on the other side of the road). We weren't giving Veronique a lift because she was doing fencing, which my cousin Juni does as well, though it's at Juni's school so no one needs to take *her*. Why we were going to Auntie Mill's I didn't know and I intended to ask, waiting while Auntie Mill's new electronic gate opened and then as she turned her burglar alarm off. We went inside, where I expected to see Clay (my other cousin), but he was at rugby practice. That just left us three, which seemed a bit weird.

'What's going on?' I said, feeling small in their huge living room.

Auntie Mill held her hands up at that and walked through to their kitchen, as if to say to my mum that it was her job to answer me. Mum took a breath. She walked over to one of the sofas, sat down and took my hand.

'It's Stephan,' she said.

I frowned. 'Are you going to the pictures *tonight*? It's only Thursday.'

'I know.' Mum shook her head. 'And no. I'm staying here.'

'Good. But what, then?'

She took a breath. 'Well, Stephan wants to

spend more time with me.'

I took that in. 'Like, maybe, Tuesdays too?'

'A lot more, actually.'

'Oh.'

'And I said I wasn't sure about that.'

'There are only so many films you can see, aren't there?'

'Right. So I suggested that, before we commit to spending a lot more time together, we get to know him a bit better. And he gets to know my family properly, too.'

'So?'

'He's coming round here.'

'Couldn't everyone have come to our house?'

'That's what I said. But Mill needs the Internet for some reason and our connection's not that good.'

'Oh. But shouldn't Dad be here too, if Stephan's getting to know us?'

'Ah,' Mum said. 'No, I . . . I think your dad's working.'

That was a shame, but they'd already met, actually. When Dad brought me home after the weekend once, Stephan was already there. He was all friendly, but Dad sort of pretended he was invisible.

'So just Stephan tonight. He's staying for supper.'

'Fine. Though . . . what *is* for supper?'

The reason I was asking was simple. When Mum was not well before Christmas, I stayed with Auntie Mill for a while and was exposed to *certain foodstuffs*. The worst were called artichokes, which take my favourite food (pizza) and make it taste REVOLTING. Auntie Mill also served me fish that was actually RAW, though the people at the takeaway place had tried to disguise that by chopping it small and wrapping it in rice. How lazy can you get?

This time, Mum answered, *she* would be cooking. She was making something special for Stephan because he's a vegetarian. That seemed okay, but when I said that I'd got something to tell her, Mum told me to save it for later because she had to 'get on'. I sighed and asked if I could watch TV. Mum agreed and I grabbed the remote control. I turned on Auntie Mill's MASSIVE screen and went into iPlayer. Whoever had used the TV last had set the volume too high, though, and Mum came rushing back through.

'Nice try,' she said, whisking the remote away.

The TARDIS whirled off without me.

I gave up on TV and went outside, where Clay's

World Cup 2018 ball was on the grass. I tried to beat my solo header record (four) but gave up because I couldn't concentrate. *The plastic, all mangled. That look on Mrs Martin's face. Me, going RED . . .* With a sigh I went back in where I did Minecraft on Mum's phone until the battery died. I rooted in her bag for her charger, understanding why she can never find her keys when I saw the lipsticks and sketchpads and her bamboo coffee cup and all the other stuff in there.

And then my eyes fell on a box. Small. Hard and square. It had a little gold star stuck on, the sight of which made me feel a *lot* better. What had Mum bought me? The box really was tiny – a new Subbuteo man? A Jacky Chapman one? And why had she bought it? Was it because I was upset over Mrs Martin? Maybe she had been listening after all. Knowing that I shouldn't look inside – but that I definitely *was* going to look inside – I began to open it. The doorbell made me jump, though, and Mum shouted out for me to answer it.

I shoved the little box back inside her bag.

It was Stephan at the door, though it took me a second to recognise him. For one thing, it was a bit odd to see him at Auntie Mill's and for another he normally wears jeans and a hoody. He had a jacket on for some reason *and* he'd flattened his hair down. And he looked nervous – had he heard about Auntie Mill's cooking? I was going to reassure him that Mum was doing it tonight but I didn't get a chance – Auntie Mill came bustling through.

'Oh,' she said, 'how lovely!'

Auntie Mill held her hands out for the bunch of flowers that Stephan was holding, which was a bit awkward as he explained that they were actually for Mum. Auntie Mill said what a shame, they were lovely flowers, and she couldn't remember the last time anyone had bought *her* any. Stephan said he found that hard to believe and Auntie Mill blushed. She said he was a real charmer and touched his arm, before pushing her hair behind her ear. Mum came out of the kitchen and glared. Mum and Auntie Mill sometimes argue and I thought they might then, actually, but the doorbell went again. This time it was Juni (my cousin).

Juni's a year older than me. That means that she calls most people 'SUCH morons', completely ignores me, and walks like the Hunchback of Notre Dame because someone seems to have Velcro-ed her eyes to her mobile phone. She'd been fencing. Apart from her phone this is *her* thing and if she'd been at our school Mrs Martin would have made a great song for her. When she wins it's good, because she breaks her ignoring-me rule to tell me about it. She describes how she lunged forward to stab an opponent or lunged back to stop a different opponent stabbing her. I don't think she'd won that day, though. Without a word she stomped in, kicked open the cellar door and bunged her mask down the stairs. She followed that by chucking her sword down after it, and then she announced that there was only one thing in the ENTIRE world that she hated more than fencing.

'And that's my ENTIRELY STUPID mum for making me DO IT!'

Then she noticed Stephan.

'DO I know you?' she said.

Stephan smiled, and held his hand out for a shake. 'Stephan,' he said. 'I think we've . . .'

'Not helpful.' Juni sighed. 'Why would I care about your name? Who *are* you?'

'Oh.' Stephan looked round, but Mum and Auntie Mill were back in the kitchen. 'I'm a friend of Janet's, Cym's mum? I've . . .'

'Well, if you are *her* friend,' Juni said, holding up a hand to stop him, 'then why aren't you at *her* house?'

'I'm sorry?'

'*If* you are *her* friend, what are you doing *here*? MUM!' Juni bellowed. 'What's this friend of Cym's mum doing in OUR house?!'

Auntie Mill came back then – and explained. Stephan was staying for supper. She smiled at Juni in a wiry sort of way, and asked if she'd *kindly* go upstairs to change. She turned back into the kitchen while Juni hissed, shaking her head until she finally noticed me. Her hands went to her hips as she pinned me with her eyes.

'*À point*,' she said.

'Sorry? "Ah . . ."?' I stared. Juni goes to a posh school and I wondered if this was something you got taught there.

Juni closed her eyes, then opened them again. '*À point*. Please tell me you know what that means.'

I thought hard but had to shrug.

'Unbelievable! It's a *way* to cook steak.'

'Cool. Thanks for telling me that.'

'Wait. I am not *just* telling you - what am I, your teacher?'

'Then . . . ?'

'*Listen*. Thursday is steak night. Tell Mum I want

mine *à point* and that she MUST NOT overdo it. Your limited brain *can* remember that?'

I was about to say yes, or at least I thought so, but Juni swivelled, marched through the living room and banged off up the stairs.

Stephan had his mouth open. 'She always like that?'

'She's nicer when she wins.'

'Right,' Stephan said, noticing that his hand was still held out and putting it down by his side.

'I mean, a bit nicer.'

CHAPTER TWELVE

I tried to tell Auntie Mill about Juni's steak. I really did, though pretty soon she was busy making 'drinkies' and talking to Stephan in the kitchen, and while she did say, 'Yes, Cym, darling,' I'm not sure she was really listening. I tried waiting for the conversation to finish but when it did I still didn't get a chance – because of Stephan.

Now, I *do* like him. As I've mentioned, he's Mum's new friend. They go to the pictures on Fridays and he comes over at the weekends sometimes too, with his girls. He fixed my bike tyre that's been flat FOREVER and he's good enough at Subbuteo to be worth playing, but not so good that he ever wins. It can be odd, though. In Greenwich Park you can tell that people think we're all together! One woman told Mum how lovely her daughters were! Mum went red. And, right then, in Auntie Mill's kitchen, Stephan made a *catastrophic* grown-up error.

'So,' he said, holding his hand over the top of his wine glass when Auntie Mill tried to pour more in, 'how was school today?'

Adults! TELL me why you ask this question! Isn't the answer *obvious*? IT WAS SCHOOL! Unless it has turned into a giant theme park (unlikely), what else is there to say? The only thing that stops me totally bugging out when I'm asked how *school was today* is that there is, as I'm sure you know, one question that is even MORE pointless. And that is: *What did you do at school today?* What did I *do*? Not only do I NOT CARE, but HOW WOULD I KNOW? I'm no longer AT SCHOOL! School has vanished into thin air, it does not exist and will not exist until I have to walk through the door next day. The only thing worse than asking us what we did at school is what Mum does: asks me what I did at school that day WHILE I AM WATCHING *THE SIMPSONS*.

Sorry, I got a bit cross there and, actually, I shouldn't have, because when Stephan asked me that day it meant

I finally got a chance to talk about Mrs Martin. I told him about the science. I went back and told him about the JE (jelly event). And I told him about my giggle. I ended with the explosion and he was amazed. I hadn't told him the importance of her bag – her most prized possession – and when I did, his mouth dropped open.

'And it wasn't you?'

'NO!!!'

'Then who was it?' he asked, and I sighed. Daisy had asked the same question and it really rang through my head now. I was baffled, though a face did come into my mind that so would have been there before Christmas. It belonged to the kid who used to be the class horror, kicking you from behind on school trips, hiding your pencil case, putting old chewing gum in your coat pocket.

Billy Lee.

But Billy and I had become friends before Christmas so it couldn't be him. *Could* it? It must have been someone in Year 6. I started to go through the names but Mum said it was suppertime.

'Juniper!' Auntie Mill called. 'Can you come and set the table, please!'

While we waited for Juni to come and help (never

going to happen) Mum went into a faff wondering where everyone should sit. Auntie Mill set the table herself, telling us that Clay was going to a friend's house. She still set six places, however, doing most of them normally, though at the head of the table she stacked up lots of glossy magazines where the plate was supposed to go. Stephan looked at me and I looked at Stephan but neither of us knew why. Then Juni came down, bumping into a chair and then a floor lamp as she walked across the living room.

'Where's my stinky brother?' she said, texting.

'Friend's house.'

'Great.' *TEXT. TEXT.* 'I'll get his steak, then.' *PING!*

'Oh,' I said, 'I don't think there's going to be—'

PING! Juni wasn't listening. 'Where's Dad?' she said, pulling her chair out with one hand. *TEXT. TEXT. TEXT. TEXT. PING! TEXT.* Stephan and I didn't know so couldn't answer, so she shouted, 'MUM? *Where's* DAD?' *TEXT. PING!*

There was quite a lot of crossness in Juni's voice and I thought I knew why. My Uncle Chris used to work all the time in this big glass building (not a greenhouse, one with computers in). He was never home for *anything*.

He'd promised to change, though, so where was he?

'Well?' Juni demanded, as Auntie Mill came through. *TEXT. TEXT. PING! PING! PING!*

'Look, love—' Auntie Mill winced, and stared at the side of Juni's bowed head. 'Daddy had to take a little trip.'

TEXT. 'Typical.' *TEXT. PING!* 'And he's not my "daddy", he's my dad.' *TEXT. PING! TEXT.* 'How little?'

'Well . . .'

TEXT. 'I mean, is he getting back soon?' *TEXT. TEXT. TEXT. TEXT.* 'Or not till after supper?'

'Neither. He's in . . .'

'His –' *TEXT* – 'office?'

'No. America.'

'*What?*' Finally, and with great effort, Juni did rip her eyes from her phone.

'New York, to be absolutely precise.'

'But he doesn't *do* that any more!' *PING!*

'I *know*, love. But some investors got in touch. Look, he's just not here. But it's only one night.'

'That's not the point!' *PING! PING!* 'My *maths* is due tomorrow!'

'I can help you with that.'

'You? I might as well ask the goldfish.'

'I beg your par—'

'Or Cymbeline.'

'Hey!'

'Well, maybe you won't have to.' Auntie Mill sighed, turning to the magazines. I noticed then that she had an iPad in her hand, which she put on top of the stack.

'Your dad said he'd be here,' she muttered. 'And he's going to be. Sort of.'

PING!

Auntie Mill started fiddling with the iPad. Juni started arguing with her again but then stopped – but not to answer any of the pings. Mum had come in with a tray. On it were three serving bowls, which Juni and I stared at as Mum set them down on the table.

'What,' Juni said, 'is *that*?'

Now, I don't often side with Juni, but I have to admit that I too wanted to know the answer to this question. You see, in the bowl that was nearest to me was what I can only describe as shiny brown sludge. The next bowl was pretty similar except that the sludge in that one was yellow. The third bowl also had sludge in, though that was green.

With bits in.

'Supper,' Mum said.

Juni shook her head. 'No,' she said. 'It. Is. Not.'

'It is! Dhal! Sort of curry. First time I've made it. That's split pea dhal with ginger, and that's lentil dhal, and that's paneer.'

'Pan—?'

'Cheese. Indian cheese.'

'That is *not* cheese.'

'Then what *is* it?' asked Mum.

'That,' Juni insisted, 'is vomit.'

'*What?*'

'From three different people by the looks of it, because vomit from only one person looks the same. Why are you putting vomit on the table, Auntie Janet? And, Mum?!' She turned to Auntie Mill, who was now waving at the iPad. 'Why can't I smell steak cooking?'

PING!!!

'!!MUM!!'

The volume of that shout from Juni finally got Auntie Mill's attention and she turned to her daughter. 'Steak?' she said.

'It's *Thursday*.'

'But Stephan's a vegetarian.'

'Why do *I* care what Stephan is?!'

'Because *he* is our guest, darling.'

'So? And why is he, anyway?'

'Auntie Janet wanted us to meet him properly. We'll do steak another—'

'Are you a *complete* imbecile?' Juni hissed. 'Or just a partial one? Steak *has* to be on Thursday to replenish my depleted protein stocks after fencing! And anyway, I'm not putting something in my body that looks like it just came out of someone else's!!'

'Juniper,' Mum hissed. 'Don't be so rude!'

'What? *You* can't tell me off.' *PING!*

'Well, someone should,' said Mum.

'What's *that* supposed to mean?' said Auntie Mill, flashing round to Mum. 'It's up to me to discipline her.'

'Then why don't you?' Mum said. (*PING! PING!*) 'The way she speaks to people! If she ever *does* actually speak to people, instead of just spending all day –' *PING! PING! PING! PING! PING! PING!* – 'OH! If

92

she were my daughter I'd—'

'Hello, everyone!' came a cheerful voice from the head of the table.

That stopped Mum and Auntie Mill. We all looked round but there was no explanation – until Auntie Mill's iPad came alive.

'Uncle Chris!' I shouted.

My Uncle Chris was on the screen, squinting into the camera. (It explained why Auntie Mill needed the Internet.) He had a napkin tucked in his shirt and behind him I could just make out tables and chairs with people at them. Wherever he was, it was noisy.

'Cymbo!' he answered, before looking round. 'Are you there? Groovy. Oh, there's lot's of you.'

'This is Stephan,' I said. 'Though normally only on Fridays.'

'Right. Welcome, Stephan. I think we've actually met, haven't we? Sorry I can't be there.' Uncle Chris held out his hand. Stephan did the same and they did a mid-air virtual shake. Then Uncle Chris turned to Juni.

'Pickle!'

'I'VE TOLD YOU NOT TO CALL ME THAT!'

'Sorry. And sorry not to be there. But this'll do, won't it?'

'No! Especially given what Auntie Janet has just served . . .'

'Are you read-eee?' said Uncle Chris, who didn't seem to be aware of what Juni was trying to say.

'*Ready?*'

'Yes, Pickle – sorry, not Pickle. Didn't think I'd let you down, did you? Can you see where I am?' He moved to the side and we got a better view of all the chairs and tables.

'Is that a restaurant, Uncle Chris?'

'Not just any, Cymbo. It's Big Al's New York Super-Steak! Best in the Five Boroughs. I've got the thirty-five-day matured grass-fed Irish rib-eye. It's *à point* and I'm ready to replenish my protein stocks. LET'S DO THIS!'

With that, Uncle Chris moved his hand up to the camera and a big silver fork came into view. On it was the juiciest, most succulent chunk of food I have EVER seen. If that was *à point*, I wanted some. Could you do pizza like that? I was about to ask but Uncle Chris's mouth came right up to the camera and the steak went in. And he chewed, after which he swooned like he was going dizzy! He nearly fell off his chair before moving back up to the camera.

'Incredible! Oh boy. But how's yours, Pick— Juni-bug? *Well?* How is it, darling?'

PING!

I cannot accurately describe the dialogue after that. There was too much shouting. Juni was loudest with:

'SO not FAIR!'

'How COULD you, Dad?!' and

'SPIT THAT OUT RIGHT NOW!!!'

as Stephan tried to say it was his fault and Mum and Auntie Mill just screamed at each other, about 1. parenting strategies, 2. ingratitude, and 3. intruding into other people's lives. (*PING!*) Uncle Chris (just his face) sat on the pile of magazines with his fork in his hand looking bewildered, while I watched it all in awe.

Until I felt something.

And it was *weird*. A weird something was happening (weirdly) at my feet.

And then my legs.

And then my stomach.

And then my chest.

A weird something that nobody noticed but me, until Uncle Chris noticed it (from New York). His expression changed from bliss to panic, and then from panic to horror as he jabbed his fork at the screen. 'RAT!' he shouted. THERE'S A RAT IN THE HOUSE, I TELL YOU!'

CHAPTER THIRTEEN

'A *rat*?' said Juni. 'Did he say "*rat*"?'

Everyone peered at the screen, trying to see what Uncle Chris was talking about.

But to my *complete* amazement, Kit-Kat the Nearly-Hamster had scampered up my legs and chest and was now sitting on my shoulder. And no one was looking at me.

How did *he* get there? Had he snuck through a gap from next door? Did he want to play Subbuteo again? I was about to ask him but first I had to get him out of sight. Fortunately no one was paying attention to me, still, so I shoved Kit-Kat down under the table, scrabbling in my pocket for one of the dried peas that were still in there. I wanted to put Kit-Kat up my jumper but one of the peas fell on the floor and he leapt down after it.

Meanwhile, Uncle Chris (in New York) was waving his arms about. And then Kit-Kat's ball control let him down! Instead of grabbing the pea, as I'd expected, he accidentally kicked it. It flew across the floor like a Harry Kane volley and he scurried after it, stopping to nibble it – in open sight! He then looked back at me, clearly wanting another. As quick as I could, I threw him one, trying to tempt him back towards me, but I was nervous and it went skidding past him. He turned and dived on it, still wide open in the middle of the floor as Uncle Chris bellowed:

'RAAAAAAAAAAAAAAAAAAAAAAAAAAAAT! It was attacking Cymbo!'

The first person to react to this new information was Mum, who didn't turn and try to protect her only son from this sudden danger. OH NO! Nor did she look around for any proof of what Uncle Chris was saying. Instead she just screamed, even louder than he'd done, so loud in fact that Auntie Mill *stopped* screaming. And then Mum jumped right up on to Stephan, using him as a kind of step as she launched herself on to the table – or not the table, quite. Instead of landing on that, Mum landed on the bowl of yellow dhal stuff, which sent the dhal flying through the air. And Juni deserves a *lot* of credit here because it really *did* look a lot like vomit now. And it looked even *more* like vomit when it stopped flying through the air and landed on Juni's T-shirt.

And her face.

And in her hair.

And you don't have to have seen *Doctor Who* to imagine what she looked like then.

So now it was Juni's turn to scream, yellow sludge dripping down her cheeks and hair. She was almost as loud as Mum, while Uncle Chris kept shouting, waving his arms and pointing at Kit-Kat, surely about to give away his location. Fortunately, though, Mum's manic treading made everything on the table wobble, and just as Uncle Chris was about to tell everyone where Kit-Kat was, his iPad tumbled head first off the pile of magazines and landed in the brown dhal. Auntie Mill dived forward to rescue him but Mum was still spinning about, during which she stepped in the green dhal—

But please don't worry! That didn't land on Juni too.

It landed on Stephan.

During all this chaos I took the chance to throw another pea to Kit-Kat, this time aiming right out into the hall so he'd disappear from sight. He scampered after it and out of the room, with me following to make sure he didn't come back in again.

Which is when I saw it.

I hadn't spotted it before, but as I picked Kit-Kat up and stared into his naughty little face I noticed a rubber band. One of those thin ones. It went right round his tummy, something I couldn't understand – until I slid it over his head.

And a little piece of folded paper fell into my palm.

And opened.

'It's Nanai,' the note said.

CHAPTER FOURTEEN

There was nothing else on the note.

Just those words.

I stared at them, all quiet and still inside – wondering whether Kit-Kat had written them. I was actually quite willing to believe that he could have done but – no – it was *definitely* Veronique's handwriting. She must have sent Kit-Kat over from her house next door. But Nanai? What had happened? Was it her breathing again? Or . . . ? I swallowed, not even able to finish my thought.

Instead I turned to the wall of sound behind me and then back to Kit-Kat, covering him up with my jumper. Then I stared at Auntie Mill's front door. I didn't want to open it. I wanted to go back into the living room.

But Veronique was my friend, wasn't she?

I didn't hesitate – I opened the front door.

It was cold outside. And dark, though it didn't stay that way for long. As soon as I moved, a light came on, something that didn't surprise me because Uncle Chris had put motion sensors and CCTV in last year after a burglar had tried to get in. It was startling, though, and scarier somehow than the dark had been was a long black shape in front of me that made me jump – until I realised it was my own shadow.

I followed it up to the road, intending to go to Veronique's door, though she might not have told her dad I was coming. So instead I turned back again, my shadow first seeming to shrink as I edged round the side of the house, then ducking in behind me like *it* was afraid. It stayed there as I emerged on to Auntie Mill's patio, where I glanced back in through the glass doors.

Mum and Juni were both on the table now, while Stephan was wiping dhal off his jacket and Auntie Mill was wiping it off her iPad, which meant that no one was looking out the window. Taking advantage of that, I hurried off down the lawn, their treehouse looming out of the darkness like it was going to jump on me.

When it didn't, I turned left and pushed my way through the bushes until I came to the secret hole that Veronique had shown me in the summer. You had to pull back a plank, which I did, though my hand connected with something slimy. A slug! After throwing that off, I got on my hands and knees and crawled through, emerging at the side of Nanai's cabin.

What would I do? What could I possibly *say* to Veronique if . . . ? I swallowed, thinking about something else that I knew about grandparents. Yes, they were great. Yes, they gave you sweets and pound coins.

But they couldn't go on doing that forever.

That thought nearly made me go back. I could tell Veronique I never got the note. Whatever Kit-Kat said, I could just deny it. I shook my head, though, and pushed on, intending to walk up their garden to their back door. But I stopped.

Nanai's light was on, a rectangle of yellow spread out in front of her cabin like a corner flag.

Not really thinking, I forced myself round to the front and stared in through the door, wondering what I'd see. A stretcher? Some ambulance people crowding round it?

No.

Nanai *was* in the cabin. But she was just in her chair, like normal, talking to Veronique and her dad. It was like someone had popped a giant balloon inside me. I closed my eyes, feeling *really* stupid about what I'd been imagining, and took a few deep breaths. Then I pushed the cabin door open and stood on the threshold, Veronique and her dad turning towards me, though Nanai didn't.

'Hello,' I said. 'How was hospital? Did they sort your breathing out?'

Nanai didn't answer. Or move. She didn't call me the famous Cymbeline *or* ask what I had to say about Jacky Chapman (or his helicopter). That was a bit weird and I glanced around, not able to spot anything actually *wrong* to explain what Veronique's note had meant. Nanai's photographs were still on the walls, the same three on the little table beside her chair. The only difference I could see was Nanai herself, who for the first time didn't have her glasses on. They were on a chain round her neck.

I turned to Veronique and took Kit-Kat out of my jumper. 'Here,' I said. 'He's better than email.'

I thought that might make Veronique smile, but it didn't. Veronique just took Kit-Kat from me and turned back to Nanai, which is when I did notice something different: the atmosphere. It was heavy. Serious, like in class after someone has REALLY been told off. And Veronique herself looked even more worried than she had at my house. This was something I couldn't understand because Nanai was *right there*. But her dad looked worried too.

'What *is* it?' I said.

Veronique bit her lip. And then she pointed at Nanai, like she had at Marcus Breen when he put a worm inside her clarinet.

'It's her,' she said.

'*Her?*' What could Nanai have done? 'Hasn't she given you any pound coins recently?'

Veronique sighed. 'No. It's *not* that.'

'Won't she play football, then? You should, Nanai, you've got real potential.'

'Cymbeline, listen.'

'Okay.'

'Nanai's *not eating*.'

'Join the club,' I said, pulling the door shut and moving further into the room. 'Neither are we.

Our dinner just puked itself up.'

'*What?*'

'I'll tell you later. What's that, Veronique?'

I was talking about the plate on Nanai's side table, which the photographs had been obscuring. A small jumble of green beans sat next to a ploughed field of mashed potato, the ridges all crispy, mince oozing up here and there like lava. It wasn't quite Uncle Chris's steak, but it was still very tempting, especially as I could suddenly smell it – which made me realise that I was starving.

'Her dinner.'

'And she won't eat it?

'No.'

'Why *not?*'

'That's the thing. She won't *tell* us.'

I turned to Nanai. 'Is it the tiny bits of carrot? I *so* get that. It's such a mean trick, but you can pick them out.'

'You don't understand,' Veronique insisted. 'She likes it that way.'

'*Really?* Then what's the problem? I'll have it if you like.'

'But we want *Nanai* to eat it.'

'Oh. Well, isn't that up to her?'

'Yes.' Veronique sighed. 'But . . .'

'I mean, she's an adult, after all. She's about as adult as you can get and still be a person.' I turned to the very old lady in the chair. 'Aren't you, Nanai?'

'We *know* that.'

'Well, then. I thought it was only kids who had to eat things they don't want. What's the point of growing up if you still have to do that? Would you like a bit of our dhal stuff instead, Nanai? I could probably scrape some off Juni for you?'

'Cymbeline!' Veronique hissed. 'It's not that she won't eat *this*. She won't eat anything.'

'Anything?'

'Nothing. She stopped eating four days ago.'

'What?'

'*Four* days ago,' Veronique said, before turning her glare back to Nanai. Who was just ignoring all of us and staring into space.

At this, I bit my lip. And I got it – why they were worried. *Four days* with no food? By then, I'd probably eat artichokes.

'Wow,' I said. 'That's . . . not good. What are you going to do?'

'Well,' said Veronique, 'actually, Cymbeline, I thought *you* might be able to help.'

CHAPTER FIFTEEN

I stared at her.

'Me?'

'Yes. Before Christmas you found out why your mum was ill, didn't you? So I thought you might be able to figure this out.'

'I see. Well . . .' I bit my lip. 'Have you done it like a train? Stephan's little girl even eats her broccoli if you do that. Not sure it would work with someone Nanai's age, though. Tried biscuits?'

'Yes.'

'Custard creams? They're your favourites, aren't they, Nanai?'

'And bourbons and digestives and Mars bars *and* KitKats.'

'WHAT?!'

'The chocolate bar. But it doesn't make *any* difference. She won't have *anything*. Just water. And the doctor says . . .'

'*What?*'

'You *know* what. What *she* said. That she wants to . . . well . . . And I can't believe—' Veronique choked. She put her hand up to her face and bit her fingers, before glaring at Nanai again. 'I can't believe that she's doing this *on purpose.*'

I studied Nanai then, and saw that she really did look different. Her arms were folded, her expression – I could see now – all determined. Closed up, like a shell. Without her glasses on, I could see the small patches of darker brown beneath her eyes, and the hundreds of little lines that crisscrossed her face like an impossible game of Pick-up Sticks. Not having her glasses made Nanai look vulnerable, both older and younger at the same time. And though her face was blank, I could tell she was upset. REALLY upset. And I thought about Mum. Before Christmas she'd been like this: sealed up. *That* had been because of a specific thing, so I looked into Nanai's eyes.

'Did something happen?' I said.

For the first time since I'd been in there, Nanai actually moved. Not a big movement: her mouth opened, almost as if she didn't mean it to, before she clamped it shut.

'What do you mean, Cymbeline?' Veronique's dad turned to me.

'Well,' I said, 'I know it's pretty quiet in here. Not much goes on, I guess. But did something happen? Four days ago? Did something happen to make you stop eating, Nanai?'

Nanai's mouth opened again. And she did turn to look at me. I smiled like I normally did – but my smile crumbled on my face. Because Nanai's shoulders rose. And she looked upset. REALLY upset, without any pretence at all that she wasn't. Like I'd said something *terrible*. It was scary and then it got scarier: her wrinkled hands clenched into fists and I thought she was going to shout at me or – worse – leap from the chair and bop me one! I'd really touched a nerve. But instead she turned to the side table. For the shepherd's pie? Again I was wrong. She reached for one of the pictures. Not the photo of her and her sister, but the one next to it, of the big ship, which she stared at for a second before jerking it up above her head.

And then, with a grunt, she flung it!

Veronique flinched. Her dad flinched too and reached out – but he was too late. The photo of the ship spun round in the air, almost in slow motion. All of us stared in amazement until – C-R-A-S-H! – it hit the wall. The frame collapsed. Glass flew. Jagged shards bounced back towards us before dropping to the floor, where they smashed again, REALLY LOUD, and skidded all round our feet. And then there was silence. Electric silence. Booming silence. It rooted us to the spot until Nanai shifted in her chair, her head bowing, her voice sounding like it came from a thousand million miles away, as – finally – she spoke to us.

'Leave me alone,' she said.

CHAPTER SIXTEEN

We didn't eat the dhal stuff. Mum bought us fish and chips instead (on the way home). We had them at the kitchen table from the paper, just her and me. I didn't like the fish much, but the chips were good. I thought about saving some for Nanai, but I knew it wouldn't work. Not the way she'd acted. Luckily, I hadn't had to explain anything about that, or Kit-Kat, because when I'd got back to Auntie Mill's they were still shouting and no one had even noticed I'd gone.

After we'd finished the fish and chips, Mum shoved the paper in the bin.

'Well,' she said, '*that* didn't go too well, did it?'

'At least Juni got her steak.'

That was true. Auntie Mill had ordered some,

though we were gone before it arrived. A nice man called Mr Uber picked us up, dropping Stephan at Lewisham station on the way. I waved as he went through the barriers but he must have been in a hurry because he didn't wave back. Mum gave my hand a squeeze and Mr Uber took us to the fish-and-chip shop near our house.

That night I lay in bed and saw it over and over again: the ship tumbling through the air after Nanai threw it. I felt the silence again and saw Veronique, staring at Nanai before suddenly turning, flinging herself out of the cabin and running back up the garden to their house, leaving her dad and me to stare after her. Then we turned to Nanai, who now had her eyes closed, her hands clenched together on her lap. Mr Chang put his hand on the back of my neck and steered me out, across the broken glass, into the night. I wanted to go and see Veronique, but he said he'd make sure that she was okay and he took me back round to Auntie Mill's instead. Before going in I turned to him, wanting to ask a question, but not wanting to at the same time.

How long can you go without eating for?

'Yes, Cymbeline?'

'Nothing,' I said, and went inside.

I saw Veronique next morning. I waited at the school gates for her until she came walking down the road from where her dad had parked the car. It wasn't that cold but she looked chilly, and pale. And tired. Worst of all she looked like she had when she'd first came to St Saviour's and didn't know anyone. Lost. Alone. I watched her, a little afraid, actually, like I used to be of her, though I pushed myself off towards her. I wanted to ask if she'd seen Nanai that morning – but Daisy Blake grabbed my arm.

Daisy pulled her stick of rock from her mouth and hissed, 'Cymbeline! Look!'

I tried to shrug myself away and turn back to Veronique, but that's not really possible with Daisy (even when she's only using one hand). So I turned the way Daisy was pointing and saw Billy Lee, laughing with Marcus Breen. I raised my eyes but Daisy shook my arm.

'Not them!' she said – and then I saw: standing by the office door, chatting to Mr Baker, was Mr Gorton. The supply teacher!

'No!' I said. 'Is Miss Phillips ill?'

Daisy shook her head.

'On a course, then? "How to use apostrophes as a

means of child torture"?'

'I just saw her.'

'So . . . ?'

'He's here for Year 3!'

I sighed with relief at that – until I realised what Daisy meant.

Mr Gorton had come in for *Mrs Martin.*

When Lance came up with his racer, Daisy wrapped her rock up, shoved it in her bag and told him what had happened.

'I'm not surprised,' he said. 'I bet she's SO gutted about her bag. Do you think she'll *ever* come back?'

That was a horrible thought and not just for the Year 3s but for all of us kids, and the teachers, *and* everyone on the Friends' Forum. Daisy's eyes opened in distress and Lance looked sick to have even mentioned it. They both started going on about what they could do. Daisy even said she had a plan, but I had Veronique to think about. Last night she'd asked for my help.

So I freed myself from Daisy's grasp and tried to get to Veronique. She'd gone past, though, was already trudging through the doors, and by the time I got upstairs the class was silent, everyone stuck into their morning reading.

'Sit down quickly, Cymbeline,' Miss Phillips said.

I didn't get a chance to speak to Veronique in class, so at first break I scanned the playground. I even went to look behind the shed with the sports stuff in, in case she was sitting there on her own. But she wasn't. I was just heading back in to look for her in the library when I was grabbed again. This time it was by Vi. She's also hard to resist and she practically dragged me over to the AstroTurf towards Lance and Daisy. They were right where Mrs Martin's bag had exploded.

'Look at this,' Daisy whispered, cutting a glance round the playground before squatting to the ground.

I thought Daisy meant the charred bit, right by her feet. But she didn't. She unzipped her bag and held it open, Vi and Lance huddling round so no one else could see. I stared inside, saw the long red stick and pulled it out.

'Cool,' I said. 'I love rock. My mum says it's a total tooth-killer, though. Where'd you get it?'

'My dad,' Daisy said. 'He went away last weekend. But it's not that. Look at *this*.'

Daisy held the bag wider and I looked in again – at a plastic box.

'What's that?'

Daisy did another look round, waiting for a Year 6 to go by. 'Detective kit.'

'Cool,' Lance said. 'You into that stuff?'

'Sort of. My dad's one.'

'Like, a policeman?'

'He used to be. He's got his own company now.'

'That investigates things?'

'Yes. He gave me this for Christmas.'

'Lucky,' I said, interested in the kit in spite of myself. The contents were shown on the box. There were glasses to disguise you, invisible-ink pens, a magnifying glass and a fingerprint pad. But Lance frowned.

'You've hardly used it!' he said.

'I know. Too dangerous.'

'*Huh?*'

'Well, on Boxing Day someone ate all the lebkuchen.'

'The what?'

'German cake things. My mum's German. Anyway, my dad loves them, so when he found out he fer-lipped. He wanted to know who'd done it and no one owned up. So guess what he did?'

'Banned TV for everyone?'

'YES!'

'Parents,' Vi said, 'are SO UNFAIR!'

'I know. Anyway, I wasn't having *that*, was I? So I got out the fingerprint kit. I took fingerprints from the lebkuchen box *and* from all the bedrooms. I proved it was my brother.'

'Johnny?'

'No. Milo.'

'Woo. Bet he was pleased.'

'Not exactly – smacked me over the head with the biscuit tin. You can still see the scar.' Daisy moved her hair out the way, and she was right.

'So you need to be careful,' I said. 'But why have you brought it?'

'*Because*,' Daisy explained, 'someone *must* have touched Mrs Martin's bag.'

'So?'

'So we'll dust it for fingerprints, then get samples.'

'From *everyone*?' I stared round the manic playground.

'Starting with our class. From their desks. If we get a match, we'll tell Miss Phillips. Yes?' Daisy's eyes were wide open and she was nodding.

Vi and Lance were nodding too, but I shook my head.

'Mrs Martin isn't in today.'

'So?'

'She probably took her bag home. That, or chucked it away. It had a massive hole in the side!'

'Aaargh, I didn't think of that. Oh! What can we *do*, then?'

Everyone was deflated but Daisy looked like she might cry. I was about to tell her that I had no idea – but I sighed. A thought had come to me. I didn't want it to, *I just wanted to think about Veronique.* But it was sitting there in my head, probably because, actually, I did need to find out who had done it too.

'Wait till lunchtime,' I said, dodging Daisy when she tried to stop me again. '*Lunchtime*,' I insisted. I saw Mrs Stebbings, in her Charlton shirt, waving at me through the kitchen window. I waved back, and after Daisy had grabbed her stick of rock back off me, I finally went to find Veronique.

We had to find out who'd blown up Mrs Martin's bag. I knew that.

But *first* I had to find out what was going on with Nanai.

CHAPTER SEVENTEEN

Veronique was in our classroom. Not reading. She wasn't even doing a crossword from *The Sunday Times* book that she has. She was just sitting in her place, staring down at the table, picking the loose thread on her jumper sleeve. I watched her through the door, a little afraid again, which made me nearly turn round and go out. But again I told myself I couldn't. I pushed the door open with my shoulder (it's started to really stick) and walked forward.

'Did you see Nanai this morning?'

Veronique turned, looking at me for a long second before nodding. 'I was supposed to be playing piano,' she explained.

'For your Grade 5?'

'Yes. But I couldn't concentrate. So I made some porridge and took it down to her. She normally *loves* porridge.'

'But she wouldn't touch it?'

Veronique shook her head. 'All she'd have was tea.'

'Did you ask again? I mean, why she wasn't eating?'

Veronique sighed. 'She wouldn't say. In fact she wouldn't say *anything*. She was just staring.'

'At the photo?'

'No. Dad picked the glass out of the frame. I tried to give it to her but she wouldn't take it.'

'Did you ask her why she threw it?'

'She wouldn't *answer*, Cymbeline.'

This time *I* sighed. 'She threw it after I asked her if something had happened to stop her eating.'

'I *know*.'

'So, *did* something happen?'

'I don't know,' Veronique said. 'And neither does Dad. We just don't *know*, Cymbeline.'

And neither did I. What *could* have happened to Nanai, there in her cabin? She couldn't even have got an email that had upset her because she doesn't use the Internet. She doesn't have a phone either so she couldn't have got a call. Or a text. There didn't seem to be *anything*, so Veronique and I sat in silence as she picked at her sleeve, looking so forlorn that I thought about picking up her hand and nibbling her finger myself. I didn't though (of course). I had another thought.

'Do you think she meant to?'

'What?'

'Throw the photo?'

'She didn't do it by accident, did she?'

'No. But I mean, did she just want to throw something? Or did she want to throw *that*?'

Veronique shrugged. 'How can we know?'

I had no idea and so we sat in silence until the rest of the class filed in.

'Right,' Miss Phillips said. 'Folders.'

We both reached for our bags and looking into mine I soon realised I must have inherited bag control problems from Mum. There were some Match Attax from Year 2, three socks (not matching), a pair of pants (not mine), two jumpers and what looked like a knee scab stuck to the bottom, but which was actually a lump of melted Skittles (I sit next to the radiator). There was also the letter Mr Baker had told us to take home after the JE (jelly event). It made me wince because I hadn't given it to Mum. She'd be cross. Seeing it stopped me, though, and not because I was going to get a telling-off. There was something about it. I didn't know what, though, so I pulled out my homework folder as Miss Phillips stepped up to the whiteboard.

'The Romans,' she wrote, in big letters, the M a bit wonky because the whiteboard's got a crack in it.

Now, we'd done a bit about Romans last term so I already knew that (a) they had fringes and (b) they walked about in squares. That morning I also learned that they actually invaded Britain twice. The first time they only stayed two weeks.

'It was probably raining,' Lance said.

The second time the Romans invaded, they stayed. And they brought toilets, money, roads, wine, central heating, togas, Christianity and rabbits.

'Though none of those are the most important thing they gave us,' Miss Phillips said. 'Who'd like to tell me what is? Not *you*, Veronique.'

The rest of us were clueless, though, so Miss Phillips had to say it:

'Writing!' She beamed, clearly expecting us to be impressed, though I wasn't. 'So we've the Romans to thank for books and plays, and poems!'

'And spelling tests,' I said, my Roman respect going

WAY down. '*Now* I know why Boudicca wanted to kill them all.'

We did the Romans until lunch, during which we also learned that they built this massive wall to keep Scotland out.

At lunch I wanted to talk to Veronique again. It had been brilliant getting to know Veronique and I could feel her sort of disappearing again, almost like she was going in reverse from when she got here. So even if we couldn't come up with anything to help Nanai, she'd at least know that I cared. There were too many people around, though, because we had first lunch sitting. Lance also reminded me that I was *supposed* to have a plan about Mrs Martin, so, with a sigh, I let Veronique go ahead of me and walked into the hall with Lance, Vi and Daisy. They went straight for our usual table by the window but I pulled them away.

'Over here,' I said.

We sat at a table near the front and I asked for Daisy's fingerprint kit.

'But you said the bag won't *be* here,' she whispered.

'It's not *for* that.'

'Then what is it for?'

'The jelly.'

Daisy grimaced. 'You can't get fingerprints off jelly!'

'I *know*. Just pass me it, will you?'

Daisy looked at me like I was mad – but she did it. And I explained. The jelly we get at school is not like home jelly. It doesn't come in bowls but in little tubs, and you get one each. *These* must come in a box . . .

'And someone must have touched the box the jelly came in, when they got out the tub to put in Mrs Martin's shoes,' I said.

'Er,' said Daisy, 'couldn't they just have saved their jelly from lunch?'

'No,' I said. 'We haven't had jelly for ages. They must have got it from the kitchens. So we'll get prints off the box it comes in, instead of from Mrs Martin's bag. Hopefully. And if they *don't* belong to Mrs Stebbings, or the other dinner ladies, we'll have solved it. Yes?'

'Yes!' they all said.

I took the kit and, holding it on my knee so no one would see, I read the instructions. Then I told Vi and Daisy to keep their eyes on the kitchen door. When the kitchen was empty, I was going to run in, dust the box of jelly tubs for finger prints – and *BINGO!*

Pretty soon, though, I realised that we had a problem.

There was *always* someone in the doorway. We've got three dinner ladies (including Mrs Stebbings) and that day they were constantly bustling about, carrying big steel tubs with steam rising out or piles of dirty plates. Even when Mrs Stebbings took a small break, she did it in the doorway, looking out at us all, her shiny face the same colour as her Charlton shirt. There was just no way past her, not even when we went up for our food. And then the problem got worse – there were only five minutes of our sitting left!

'We need a distraction,' Daisy said.

With that, she gritted her teeth and pulled out some strands of her hair. I had no idea what she was doing until she shoved them in Lance's sticky toffee pudding.

'Hey!' he snapped, but Daisy pointed at the hatch.

'Go and complain. Ask for another one.'

'I should just eat yours!'

'It's so Cym can sneak into the kitchens!'

Lance was still VERY annoyed but he understood what she meant. Muttering that he could have put HIS hair in HER pudding, he walked over. But it was no use. While Lance was talking to one of the other dinner ladies, Mrs Stebbings never left the doorway.

'Didn't even give me any more,' Lance sulked when

he got back. 'She just pulled your hair off and poured more custard on.'

Daisy sighed, though she didn't care about Lance's pudding. She was really frustrated now. She looked round and her eyes fell on Veronique, who was sitting at the next table on her own.

'Come and sit with us,' Daisy said.

Veronique looked down at her plate. 'No thanks. I don't really . . .'

'Come and *sit* with us,' Daisy insisted, nearly dragging Veronique over the benches. Veronique had no choice but to agree, swinging her legs over and putting her apple down in front of her. An apple – instead of Mrs Stebbings's STP! It showed how miserable she was. Not that Daisy noticed.

'We need a *plan*,' she announced.

'A . . . ?'

'*Plan*. We've *got* to find out who's doing things to Mrs Martin. Well?' Daisy was staring at her but Veronique didn't reply. It was like each of Daisy's words was actually painful – she so just wanted to be by herself. 'Don't you *care*?' Daisy added.

'Ye-yes,' Veronique stammered, 'but . . .'

'What?'

'Well, you see, I've got . . .'

'*What?*'

'I mean . . .' Veronique looked down at the table again. 'Other things. To . . . think about. I'm sorry . . .'

'What other things?'

'Well . . .'

'Don't you see how important this is?'

'Of course I do. But you see . . .'

'See what? How could you be so *self*ish?'

'Daisy . . .' I started.

'No, Cym. She's *really* brainy. She could think of something. A plan. But she *won't*. It's pathetic.'

'It's not. She . . .'

But Daisy wouldn't listen. She spun back round to Veronique. 'You hate PE, don't you?' She had a point. Veronique *was* always trying to get out of it. 'You weren't up on the heath, *were* you?'

'I had a cold.'

'So it could have been you! Is *that* why you won't help? Did *you* do it? And –' Daisy's eyes burst open – 'you'd be clever enough to make her bag explode!! Are YOU doing it all?'

Daisy was leaning in on Veronique. Veronique stared back, not knowing what to say, scared and

128

disbelieving, while I started to tell Daisy not to be an idiot. But then Marcus Breen came up with Billy Lee.

'Siri,' he said, 'if something belongs to your group of people, whose is it?'

Veronique looked confused. She just wanted Marcus to go away. So she said, 'Ours.'

Marcus high-fived Billy. 'You said ours! Now maths: if there are six art groups and the first is A Art, and the second is B Art, what's the sixth one?'

'Who cares?'

'I do. *Tell me.*'

Veronique was exasperated, looking this way and that like a cornered rabbit. She stared at Marcus, about to answer, clearly hoping it would make him leave.

But she stopped.

'Look,' Marcus insisted, sticking his face right into hers, 'the *first* class is A Art. So the sixth one MUST be . . . ?'

He was trying to tease the answer out of her. But Veronique's neck had gone rigid and her eyes hard.

'Go. Away.'

'But you nearly said it, Siri. Come on!'

'I told you to GO AWAY!' Veronique shouted. And our class genius (who plays piano and clarinet and violin, and does the Rubik's cube faster than I can say 'does the Rubik's cube') SHOVED Marcus Breen in the chest!

Marcus shook his head. He was hardly able to believe it – until Billy shoved him back towards Veronique. He went right into her, which wasn't really Marcus's fault, but Veronique wasn't having it. She shoved him again. This time it was much harder and should have sent him flying into the table behind. But instead he went into . . .

Mr Gorton, the supply teacher, knocking the tray in his hand so it was suddenly *not* in his hand, making the plates spin off like flying saucers until they crash-landed on a table of Year 2s.

Oh no.

Meanwhile, Marcus jumped back at Veronique, trying to attack her. But she was too quick, probably due to her fencing classes. She grabbed Marcus's hair and shook his head, while Marcus wailed, Mr Gorton tried grabbing at them, and Miss Phillips started to barrel towards us from the queue. She got hold of Veronique and then the dinner ladies piled in too. I tried stop it all, but Lance had grabbed my arm and before I could pull it away Daisy and Vi had both grabbed me too and spun me round to the kitchen door.

The *empty* kitchen door!

Three seconds later, I was through it.

Three seconds after that, I was on my hands and knees, pushing aside two drip buckets.

Three seconds after *that*, I was pulling a box from the shelf, the word **JELLY** printed in BIG letters on the side.

And three seconds after *that*, footsteps were thumping up behind me.

'Igloo!' the voice boomed. 'What on earth do you think you're DOING, BOY?'

CHAPTER EIGHTEEN

And now I think I should probably tell you a little bit about Mr Baker (our new head teacher). Before Christmas, I got a *tiny bit* fighty on a school trip. I had to go and see Mrs Johnson (our last head teacher). The 'little chat' she gave me was terrifying, even though she ended it by giving me a hug.

Something told me – as I looked up at Mr Baker – that the next five minutes were going to be worse.

There's just something *about* him, and it's not simply that no one wanted Mrs Johnson to retire, which we didn't. She was strict but in a sparkly sort of way. The school felt right when she was there and wrong when she wasn't, like if the Queen's not at Buckingham Palace and they don't fly the flag outside.

She was in charge in a way that made you feel safe, made you feel like someone was looking after the whole school – and everyone in it.

By contrast, Mr Baker looks like he's always thinking about something else. If he's with the parents, he sort of turns on his attention, but when they're not around it's like we kids are a bit, well, *in the way*. He walks past without saying hi, which Mrs Johnson never did, and he talks on his phone as if it's a weekend and we're actually not *there*. In assemblies he's sort of rushed, but in Praise Assembly, when the parents are there, he's slower, and smilier, going on about how we're a community, that a school is far more than its buildings and space, which he says are actually irrelevant. It's almost like we've got two Mr Bakers – and I knew which one was standing in front of me now.

I turned and stared up at our head teacher, who had his arms folded, a ring on his little finger glinting in the light from the window. Realising that my hands were still on the jelly box, I pulled them back, everything inside me clenching.

'D-doing . . . ?' I stammered.

'You heard me! DO-ING. What are you DO-ING?

There have been some dreadful things happening in this school and it seems that I've just stopped another one. WELL?'

'What? No! Please – it wasn't me. Any of it. Or this. I . . .'

'YES?' said a voice, though it didn't belong to Mr Baker. It was coming from behind him and was louder, and EVEN MORE ANGRY.

And that's when I saw Mrs Stebbings. She took in Mr Baker, none too pleased to see him there, and then she took in me. She barged past Mr Baker, an action that might have sent him flying if he hadn't just about jumped out of her way.

And her eyes went as wide as dinner plates.

'What,' she wanted to know, 'are *you* doing in here?'

I wanted to answer but my mouth was too dry. I couldn't speak. I licked my lips to try again but Mr Baker beat me to it.

'I saw him!' he exclaimed.

'Doing what?'

'Dashing in. He used that commotion outside as cover.'

Mrs Stebbings jerked upright. 'Did he? What on

earth *for*, Mr Baker?'

'Isn't it obvious?'

'Not to me! Cymbeline is a fine young man and . . .'

'Well, he's clearly stealing, isn't he?'

'STEALING?!' Mrs Stebbings rounded on Mr Baker as if he were mad. She started to tell him this in fact – but then she saw the jelly box. And her expression changed, the outrage and disbelief turning to shock.

'What?' she said. 'My sticky toff not good enough for you?'

'It is!' I insisted.

'Doesn't look like it.'

'Well, it is. I promise. It's my second-favourite food item of all time! And if you could put it on pizza it would be first! I *wasn't* stealing.'

'But he's caught you red-handed!' said Mrs Stebbings. 'Though, Mr Baker, I would prefer it if *no one* came into my kitchens uninvited, thank you. Cymbeline Igloo, I'd NEVER have believed it!'

'But I wasn't. I . . .'

'What, young man? Well? WELL?' boomed Mrs Stebbings, her hands going into fists which clamped themselves on to her sides like the FA Cup.

And then both she and Mr Baker glared at me.

And so I said it. I had to. Leaving out Daisy, Lance and Vi, and letting the head teacher and the head dinner lady think the fingerprint kit was *mine*, I told them all about trying to find the *person who'd put blue jelly in Mrs Martin's shoes*. 'And therefore the person who must have exploded her bag,' I finished.

'Which wasn't you?'

'No! I love Mrs Martin. We all do. I was trying to find out who it really WAS. And . . .'

'Yes?'

'If I was stealing the jelly, I'd hardly bring a fingerprint kit, would I? Well?'

Mr Baker's expression wavered a bit at that and I was pleased. It had been the right thing to say. In contrast, however, Mrs Stebbings looked EVEN MORE angry. Of the two of them, I'd have thought Mrs Stebbings would have been the easiest to persuade. I *really* like her and I *know* she likes me. But this time she was FURIOUS.

'Think someone could have got into MY kitchen, do you? To steal my jelly? Door's always locked.'

'But I got in, didn't I?'

'Doesn't matter. That was a fluke. Anyway, here I

am, aren't I? And, Cymbeline, how many years have you known me?'

I didn't know what she meant. Or why she was asking. 'Since I've been here?' I tried.

'Four years, then?'

'Yes, but . . .'

'So you know who I support, then.'

'*Support?*' spluttered Mr Baker. 'What's that got to do . . .'

Mrs Stebbings turned to Mr Baker and scowled. 'Yes,' she insisted, 'support. Well?'

'Charlton,' I said.

'Of course! Fifty-nine years, woman and girl. Had a season ticket for more than forty, haven't I?!'

'Well, that is of course impressive, Mrs Stebbings, but what has it got to do with . . . ?'

'*Everything*. What *colour* do we play in, Cymbeline?'

'Colour?'

'You heard.'

'Red!'

'Of course. And which team plays in . . . *blue*?'

'Chelsea,' I said. 'And Leicester. Then of course there's Milw—'

'I BEG YOUR PARDON!?'

'*Sorry!*' I said, swallowing the name of our nearest and deadliest rivals as quick as a wizard who won't say 'Voldemort'. 'The Team Who Must Not Be Named?' I corrected.

'**Exactly!**' bellowed Mrs Stebbings. '**And** *you* come in *here*, looking for *blue* jelly? BLUE jelly, in MY kitchen? Never! What on earth do you think Jacky Chapman would say?!'

CHAPTER NINETEEN

The answer to Mrs Stebbings's question was that I *didn't know*. Jacky Chapman still hadn't replied to my letter about my Person Project. What I did know, then, was that whoever was targeting Mrs Martin had brought their own (blue) jelly into school to put in her shoes. That should have been really annoying – it meant there was nothing to fingerprint, so no way now to find out who was doing it. As far as Mrs Martin was concerned, it still could have been me!

For the moment though I was a little more concerned about my immediate prospects, but two things went in my favour.

1. Once I'd apologised to Mrs Stebbings, she said, 'Well, we'll say no more about it.'

2. Although I could tell Mr Baker was going to be tougher, I got lucky: just at that point Miss Phillips came in. After taking a curious look down at me she told Mr Baker he was needed. He shook his head and hurried out while I sighed with relief, my heart smashing around in my ribcage.

'Hop it,' said Mrs Stebbings, with a shake of her head. 'Blue jelly, indeed!'

I hopped it.

Daisy was still in the hall. 'Did you get them?' she said. I shook my head, told her what had happened, and gave her back her fingerprint kit.

'Then what are we going to do?' she asked.

I wanted to help. I really did. But I had to go and find Veronique. Because it had come to me: I knew what must have happened to Nanai! No Internet, no phone . . . there was only one possible explanation.

Veronique, however, was in with Mr Baker about the pushing Marcus thing. And when I realised that, I winced. Veronique might not be the easiest of pupils to have around if you're a teacher. She asks questions ALL the time, and corrects Mrs Phillips if she gets a date a bit wrong or can't quite remember something. But she's never been really told off. Mr Baker didn't *know* her and he'd go mad. I sighed, wanting to go and stand up for her, to tell him she'd been provoked and that was why she was fighting. *And* that she had stuff going on at home. I even got as far as the office door, but just when I'd found enough courage to knock, Miss Phillips came out.

'Run along,' she said. 'And pronto if I were you.'

I did move away from the door but I hung around in the corridor, wanting to see Veronique when she came out. But two minutes later the bell went.

'Cymbeline,' said Miss Phillips, and I turned. She'd waited for me. She stepped aside, raised her eyes, and there was nothing for it but to go on past her.

It was more Romans after lunch, which they ate lying down. Mum would have shouted 'Table manners!' and generally freaked out, so lucky for them that she's modern.

Veronique's chair stayed empty.

She didn't even come for guided reading. *War and Peace* sat abandoned at her place until I picked it up and turned to the front page, though I was really just using it to look out the window at the office door. When Veronique came out, I was psyched – but then I saw her mum with her, who must have must have come back from her music tour. She must have been called in to school, which meant that it was *really* serious. And they didn't turn back towards the school. They walked out through the gates, pushing them open because the green button's stopped working. I stared, willing Veronique to turn round, which – amazingly – she did, though she just stared at me before getting into their Volvo.

Miss Phillips's voice cut through the silence. 'Concentrate, please, Cymbeline, though good choice of reading, I must say. *Another* Tolstoy fan! I'm very much looking forward to your book report. You've only about another eight hundred pages to go, by the look of it.'

Wonderful.

Five minutes later I sneaked another glance out the window but there was a gap in the line of cars on the road, like Mrs Martin's gappy smile.

After guided reading we got our Person Project books out. Everyone started writing, but I couldn't do anything, which Miss Phillips noticed.

'Still no reply?' she asked, appearing at my side.

'No.'

'Well, bit of a long shot, wasn't it? I know you wanted something more personal. And a ride in his helicopter. But there's not much we can do, is there?'

'Doesn't matter.'

'Oh?'

'I'm not doing Jacky Chapman now.'

Miss Phillips laughed. 'Who, then? Neymar? Ronaldo?'

'This person's more amazing than a footballer.'

'What's his name, then?' she asked.

'*She*'s called Nanai,' I said.

CHAPTER TWENTY

Let me explain.

I mean, I still loved Jacky Chapman and OBVIOUSLY I still wanted him to fly to school in his helicopter and take me off in it to a game.

But I also HAD to think of a way to speak to Nanai. I wasn't going to mess around. I was just going to ask her: did she get a letter, four days ago – no, *five* days ago now? A letter that had, for some reason, upset her?

That was my idea, and the more I thought about it, the more I thought it *had* to be the case. What else could have happened? She didn't have a phone, and she didn't have Internet. If someone had gone round to see her, Veronique or her parents would know about it. It *had* to be a letter – NOTHING ELSE made sense.

There was no way I could ask Mum to take me round there, though – Veronique's mum had looked SO cross earlier. Veronique was bound to be grounded. So would Mum take me to Auntie Mill's again? If so, I could play football in the garden and go through the fence, or even throw something at Veronique's window from Auntie Mill's spare room and go across on her loft ladder.

But Mum said no.

It was after school. We were outside on the heath, everyone running around with footballs, queuing up at the ice-cream van or whizzing about on bikes. All because – YES – it was Friday. But I didn't care about that. I crossed my fingers behind my back, and asked Mum about Auntie Mill.

But she shook her head.

'Why not?' I moaned.

Mum shrugged. 'Mill won't return my texts. Probably annoyed about the dinner. Honestly, my sister is SO touchy.'

'But can't you just say sorry?'

Mum stared at me. '*Me!?* What for?'

'Er, for telling her how to bring up her children? Trashing her house with dhal? Not to mention their iPad?'

'Can't see that it was my fault, not if they can't keep rodents out of their home. Though I am getting the iPad fixed. Why do you want to go round there anyway?'

'To see Nanai.'

'Really? What for?'

I thought about explaining, but it was too complicated. 'I mean, Clay's drone,' I said. 'He's been promising me a go for ages.'

'Well, maybe if I manage to get the iPad mended. Let's go and see if it's ready, shall we?'

That was the best I was going to get, so I agreed, hoping that Mum might be able to take the iPad round if it was mended. I thought she just meant popping into Blackheath Village for it, though, so when I realised where she *did* mean, I groaned.

We were going to Lewisham Shopping Centre.

Now, the problem with shopping centres is, of course, the shops. Without these they would be good places where you could go skateboarding or do Nerf battles when it's raining. One or two shops would be okay, but there are just SO many, something parents USE. Example: buying Lance's birthday present from Argos should have taken five minutes.

And it did take five minutes.

Afterwards, though, Mum said we just had to 'nip' into WHSmith for some ink, 'nip' into the pound shop for some tea lights, 'nip' into TK Maxx to see if they had any trainers, and then 'nip' into M&S, a 'nip' that turned out to be hours long because she forced me to try on clothes (a pointless exercise anyway because she always buys them MASSIVE, not seeming to care that before I grow into them I spend two years looking like a garden gnome). After THAT, I had to wait *even* longer while she tried clothes on herself, something REALLY embarrassing because it was bras. 'I don't know which is nicest!' I'd said, after the sixth one. 'And you wear them underneath things, what does it MATTER what they look like?'

But this time was even worse.

I thought we could just get the iPad back and take it round to Auntie Mill's. The man in the repair shop said the iPad wasn't quite ready, though, and to pop back in a bit, which made Mum look me up and down. And up again. She then took me for what she described as a 'hairCUT' but which turned out to be a 'hairMASSACRE'. I was then forced to itch my way round Sainsbury's, which took even longer than usual because Mum kept inspecting every single product for E-numbers (her new thing).

Soon it felt like there were red ants underneath my collar, so to hurry her up I said, 'Don't you need to get ready?'

'For what?'

'The cinema?'

'Oh,' Mum said, swallowing and looking away from me. 'No. I . . . I don't think I'm going tonight.'

'But it's Friday. Isn't there anything you want to see?'

'Not . . . really. Much rather stay in with you, Cym.'

Mum gave me a quick smile but then pulled her phone out and checked the screen, before shoving it back in her bag.

At the repair shop the iPad was finally ready.

'What *was* that stuff?' the man asked.

He wanted Mum to check that the apps were still working but we didn't have Auntie Mill's password. Mum called her and, after she'd left a message, Auntie

Mill *did* call back. Mum unlocked the iPad and it all did seem to work. Mum carried on talking to her while she paid the man, looking cross at first until it *seemed* like she and Auntie Mill had made up. She laughed and I was glad because it meant that I *might be able to go round*. Mum laughed harder.

'It's Uncle Chris,' she said, after asking Mill to hold on a sec. 'When he shouted "rat", the people in Big Al's Super-Steak thought he meant in *there*. There was a mass stampede for the door! Now he's been banned for life!'

I thought *that* was pretty funny. Mum looked a bit more serious afterwards, though, and turned away, saying something to Auntie Mill about someone not calling her all day. I was frustrated, just wanting to know if *Auntie Mill would let me go round*. There was nothing I could do about that, though, so I checked the screen of the iPad for Minecraft. Auntie Mill didn't have it (some people are so weird) but Flow Free was there. I wandered out into the shopping centre and found a bench. I sat on it and moved my finger, about to click on the Flow Free icon, when something caught my eye. It was a folder, a few icons along, up at the top left corner of the screen.

CCTV

I knew Auntie Mill had CCTV. After the burglars tried to get in, Uncle Chris had insisted on installing it himself – he loves gadgets. He showed me how it worked because Juni and Clay weren't interested. The camera was mounted above their door, sending pictures to their iPad to record them. Uncle Chris asked me to pretend to be a burglar and then we both watched as I snuck about. The camera only started when there was light, though, which is why they've got the automatic ones that came on when I went outside yesterday. Why this had taken my attention from Flow Free I didn't know.

Until it occurred to me.

If Nanai *had* got a letter that made her stop eating, SOMEONE *MUST* HAVE DELIVERED IT. It can't have been the postman, because Veronique or her dad would have seen it, and neither of them could think of ANYTHING that might have happened to Nanai.

So someone else must have brought it, probably when everyone else was out.

I glanced into the shop.

Mum was still talking.

So I clicked on the CCTV folder.

CHAPTER TWENTY-ONE

The folder was full of little files with dates underneath.
The latest one, I could see, was yesterday. After a quick
glance into the shop again, I opened it, and immediately
saw Auntie Mill's road. In the bottom corner was
the time – 6.34 a.m. I was thrilled, though I couldn't
quite see how much of the pavement the camera had
captured. To find out, I moved the cursor forward until
8.15, which is when I knew Veronique left for school.
And YES – as I'd been hoping – the camera *did* show
her house. And there was Veronique, with her dad,
hitching her bag over her shoulders as she started to
walk down the road! So if someone had come to see
Nanai, Auntie Mill's CCTV camera would show them!

Trying to swallow my excitement I counted

backwards through the days. Nanai had stopped eating five days ago now. That's what Veronique had said. And that would have been . . . Sunday. Glancing up *again* I closed the file for yesterday and found the one for Sunday. When I opened it the time showed 6.39 a.m., so I scrolled forward, looking for people. At 7.12 a dog walker came into view. She didn't stop, though her dog did deliver something, right in the middle of the pavement (disgusting).

I scrolled on again and at 7.35 a car went by. At 7.48 another dog walker went by (and trod in the delivery from the first dog). At 8.06 a boy walked past eating crisps, before throwing the packet on the floor (disgusting). I shook my head, trying not to get demoralised by the behaviour of the human race, and then I saw some cyclists, lumpy dads stuffed into Lycra clothes like Christmas stockings. I went on again until a red car came into view. I was about to ignore it but it slowed down and parked. No one got out, though, so I went on again until I saw Veronique coming out of her house with her dad. Not to go to school, of course, because it was Sunday. She had her violin case and her fencing bag, which she put in the boot of their car before they drove away.

So now they were all out: Veronique, her dad, and her mum. Nanai was there on her own.

I scratched my head and stared at the time at the bottom of the screen: 9.45. Knowing that I might have the whole day to trawl through, I sighed, about to move the film on again. But just as my finger stretched forward for the time bar, I saw a movement. It was the car, the red one that had stopped.

The door was opening. Taking my finger away, I let the film run on. And a man got out. To begin with I was disappointed – he didn't look like a delivery person. He was really tall and wore a suit and tie, buttoning up his jacket as he looked at Veronique's house. There was something about him that made me frown, but before I could work out what it was the man moved. He walked forward, to the wooden door at the side of Veronique's house that leads down to their garden.

And to Nanai's cabin.

Yes!

Trying to contain my excitement I watched the man open the door and walk through it. So there HAD been a visitor – a visitor who'd waited until everyone else was out.

So excited about being proved right (sort of), I glued

my eyes to the screen as two minutes went by. Then three, four – until I realised that – *doh* – I could move the film forward. I did, fairly slowly, so as not to miss anything, until the side door re-opened.

And the same man came out.

Once again, I squinted at him. There was still something about him I couldn't quite grasp. He seemed normal enough, though once again I thought that he just didn't look like he'd delivered something. Confused, I watched as he strode back to his car, not getting in but leaning against it while he lit a cigarette (disgusting). He sucked on it, looking miserable for some reason, while I shook my head. I was just about to go back to when he'd first got out the car but my heart leapt into my throat.

'What are you *doing*?' Mum said.

Mum had come out of the shop. Nearly dropping the iPad, I looked up. 'Er . . . testing Auntie Mill's apps.'

'Oh,' Mum said, frowning at the screen. 'Well, you really should have waited for me. Who knows *what* my sister's got on there.'

'Sorry.'

'It's fine. Though . . .' Mum peered over my shoulder. 'What *is* this?'

I shrugged. 'Not *really* sure,' I said. 'I *think* it's their CCTV.'

'You're right.' Mum nodded, put her shopping bags down, and sat on the bench. 'Bit paranoid if you ask me. It's like Fort Knox, that place. The more you have, the more you have to worry about. PS4s, drones, Xboxes, iPads . . . Oh—' Mum squinted at the screen. Then she budged up towards me.

'What is it?' I said.

'That's funny.'

'What is?'

Mum didn't speak until I nudged her. 'Sorry. But . . .'

'What?'

'Well –' Mum laughed – 'this is Mill's CCTV, right?'

'Right.'

'And that car's parked outside Veronique's house?'

'Yeah.'

'Then what's Graham doing there?'

'*Graham?*'

Mum took the iPad off me and squinted at it. Then she pointed at the man who was leaning against the car. 'What's he doing in Blackheath?'

'What's *who* doing in Blackheath?'

'They live in Greenwich, don't they?'

'Who do?'

'Yes, I'm sure they do.'

'*Who*, Mum?'

'Down by the station, just behind St Alfege, I'm sure.'

'*Who* live in Greenwich near the station?!'

'Sorry.' Mum smiled and handed the iPad back. 'Daisy's in your class, isn't she?'

'*Daisy?*'

'Blake. *You* know *her*.'

'Of course I know her. But why *on earth* are you asking?'

'Because,' Mum said, leaning forward to the iPad again and pinching the screen so that the man's face totally filled it, 'that's her dad, isn't it?'

CHAPTER TWENTY-TWO

Daisy from my class's **DAD**?

Going to see Veronique's **GRANNY**?

SECRETLY?

On **SUNDAY**?

The day she stopped **EATING**?

????????????????

!!?WHAAAAT?!!

??????????????????

CHAPTER TWENTY-THREE

Supper was vegetable lasagne (from Sainsbury's). Mum had made sure it didn't have any E-numbers, and in my opinion it could have done without the vegetables too. I picked them out and thought of Nanai.

And Daisy Blake.

And her dad.

I never thought I'd be saying this, but it was a bigger brain squeeze than *apostrophes*.

I *had* to speak to Veronique.

There was no way I could do it that night, though. I couldn't even go to Auntie Mill's because Uncle Chris had come back and they were having a family night. Could I go round and see Daisy?

'Too late,' Mum said. 'And you'll see her in the morning anyway.'

That was true. So I just sighed, trying to fight my impatience. And be nice to Mum. She seemed miserable, even during the film we put on (*Calamity Jane*, her favourite). She kept checking her phone and putting it down again. When the film finished, she did it one more time, then sighed and put me to bed. When she'd gone, I yawned, remembering the little box I'd seen in her bag, but it was too late now. Perhaps she'd give me it tomorrow.

Mum lets me walk up to the heath on my own on Saturday mornings. That morning it was cold (my ears especially, after the hairmassacre), with massive, low clouds that swept across the sky like some migrating buffaloes I'd seen on David Attenborough. They were a bit scary for some reason so I ran all the way, impatient to get there anyway. I only stopped when I passed our school because the same men I'd seen after the JE (jelly event) were there again. This time they were pointing lasers around. I wondered again if they were police, but they didn't look like it and, anyway, Billy Lee's dad was talking to them. I left them there and went to where we play.

And looked for Daisy.

Daisy wasn't there yet. Vi was, standing next to her dad and our other coach, Dave, as they set up the goals. Seeing Vi made my heart sink. It's not that I don't like her, but she was doing rainbow flicks and they were *really good*. We had the start of the Lewisham Cup in ONE week's time. We'd been training for it for *years* as it only starts in Year 4. For all those years I'd been sure I'd be on the team – but Vi keeps getting better! And so does Daisy, who's a defender you SO wouldn't want to mess with! What's more, they both do something we boys HATE – they actually PASS the ball. Vi's dad and Dave really clap when they do that and recently I've had doubts about my place. I SO didn't want to start on the bench. We don't even *have* a bench. You just have to stand around on the halfway line with your coat on.

I shook that thought away, though, and saw more kids walking over from Blackheath Village. It was just Billy, though, then Lance and Darren Cross. More came – *but not Daisy*. I was beginning to think she might not be coming at all when she walked up from the other direction with Elizabeth Fisher, who'd never been before. Another girl! If she passed the ball too, then we boys were toast! I shook my head and was about to run up to Daisy when I stopped.

The girls hadn't come on their own.

The parents were all chatting. Normally, some hang around during training, pretending not to love it when they have to kick the ball back to us. Most drop their kids off and come back at the end, though, to watch the matches. Daisy's dad does this – and he was there. He was in a fluorescent running kit, which made me realise *why* I hadn't recognised him on the CCTV. I only *ever* see him at football and he looked SO different in a suit, so much so that if Mum hadn't identified him I don't think I ever would have. Talking to him would be even better than talking to Daisy, so, before I could wimp out, I sprinted over.

'Mr Blake!' I called out.

'*Yes?*' he said, turning and fixing me with a frown, while at the same time fiddling with his watch. 'Cymbeline, isn't it? What can I do for you, young man?'

Do? I had no idea. I wanted – of course – to ask him what he'd been doing at Veronique's house last Sunday. But I couldn't do that, could I? 'Er . . .'

'Spit it out, then.'

'Well . . .'

'What is it? My daughter's hand in marriage?'

'NO!?'

'Only joking. Answer would be yes, though. To *anyone*. But I haven't got all day.' He looked up from his watch. 'Need to see if I can beat Seb Coe's mile record.'

'Really?'

'No. A joke. So?'

'Sorry, it's just . . .'

'*Just?*'

'Well –' I took a breath – 'you're a policeman, aren't you?'

'Where did you get that mad idea?'

'Daisy. She told me.'

Mr Blake laughed. 'Well, like most of her homework, it's sort of right. Why are you asking?'

Why *was* I asking? 'I, er, thought, *maybe*, that's something I might do.'

'Need to grow a bit.'

'When I'm older, I mean.'

'Of course. Well, I *was* one. Hung up my handcuffs and now I investigate things myself. That answer your question?'

'Not quite. What *sort* of things do you investigate?'

Daisy's dad rubbed his chin. 'Divorce work's a lot of it.'

'Sorry?'

'Ah. If a husband – or wife – thinks that their wife – or husband – is . . . doing something they shouldn't, I try to find out.'

Was Nanai doing something she shouldn't? With someone's husband or wife? I didn't think so. 'Is that all?'

'*Nooo* . . . Lot of online security stuff these days.'

'Online . . . ?'

'Beefing up firewalls, that sort of thing.'

'Anything else?'

'Workplace fraud.'

'Work . . . ?'

'Fella says he's too ill for an honest day's toil but then I find out he's been snowboarding in the French Alps.'

'And is that it?'

'Just about.'

Drat. He *couldn't* have been seeing Nanai about divorce work. She's not married. Firewalls? Nanai's cabin is made of wood, there's no way she'd have one of those. And I was certain that Nanai didn't go snowboarding in the French Alps or anywhere else.

I sighed, about to thank Mr Blake, when he said, '*Sometimes* we get more interesting stuff.'

'Like what?'

'Buildings security. Finding people.'

Finding people? 'Like, if they've gone missing?'

'No. Missing persons, the police do that.'

'What, then?'

'Well, we . . .' Daisy's dad paused. And looked a bit sad. 'People try to find people from their past.'

'What kind of people?'

'Could be anyone.' He shrugged. 'Someone might have lost touch with a friend. Or a work mate. Or someone who . . .'

'*Yes?*'

Again he paused, and I stared at him. He stared back, suddenly a little suspicious. 'Let's just leave it at that, shall we?'

'Okay, but do you always find them?'

'Sadly, no. Though . . .'

'Yes?'

'Well . . .' He smiled to himself, and shook his head. 'Sometimes, finding people is actually worse, believe it or not. Worse than if I hadn't found them.'

I wanted to ask him what he meant by that, but he turned and I watched him lope off towards Greenwich Park.

And I thought about what he'd said – but Vi ran over to show me her kick-ups. She used BOTH feet and beat my current record by SIX, though there was no way I was going to tell her that. I was about to go over and find Daisy but she came over too. Her stick of rock was all pointy now and there was quite a lot of white showing. She still had about half left, though. After giving it a lick she scooped up Vi's ball, headed it, then caught it on the back of her neck!

Wonderful.

And then, before I could ask Daisy about her dad, the coaches called us all in.

I sighed but there was nothing I could do. I ran over behind Vi, as Daisy put her rock away. Then (after the usual REALLY HILARIOUS haircut comments) we did our TOTALLY boring and TOTALLY pointless stretches. I mean, if you start touching your toes during a match, the other team's going to score loads, aren't they? After that we did two-on-twos, which were more fun, though I wasn't with Daisy so I couldn't speak to her, and I didn't get a chance during corner drill either. When we had a six-a-side match at the end, she was on the other team. There was no point even thinking about Nanai, so I concentrated on the game, even remembering to pass the ball (twice). The first time, Lance was so surprised that it went behind him. The second time, I was in on goal but it was at an angle, so instead of going for glory I knocked it to Billy Lee in the middle. When he scored the **SO EASY** tap-in he demonstrated *why* we never pass. Did he thank me? No – he slapped the front of his Hazard shirt and wheeled around like it was all *his* doing. His dad had come over from the school and he bellowed, 'GO ON, MY SON!' without even noticing *me*. Not that I cared – I *just* wanted the final whistle to come. And when it did, I *finally* ran over to Daisy.

'Your dad,' I panted, as Daisy did a rainbow flick that was just as good as Vi's. 'Your dad!'

'I've already *asked* him.'

'You have?!'

'About Mrs Martin. And he won't *do* anything. He says we shouldn't either. He thinks we should leave it to the teachers.'

'Oh,' I said. 'Well, that's a shame. But I didn't mean that.'

'What did you mean?'

I hesitated, about to tell her about Veronique and Nanai – but I remembered what she'd been like to Veronique on Friday. I knew I should be really mad at her, but I didn't have time for that.

'Does he talk about his work? The things he's investigating?'

'Are you kidding? It's all Top Secret. Client confidentiality, he calls it. He won't even tell my mum, and he's got an office at home that he keeps locked when he's not in it.'

Double drat.

'Anyway,' Daisy went on, 'we've got to think of another plan for Mrs Martin! Though it'll have to wait till Monday I suppose.'

'Will it?'

'If you're going away for the weekend.'

That was a strange thing for Daisy to say and I stared at her. 'If I'm going . . . ?'

'Away. Like Lance.'

Lance was going cycling with his club, but why was Daisy asking if I was going away too? I didn't get the answer until I realised that she was looking over my shoulder. And I turned round and saw Mum. She comes to watch the matches at the end, and to pick me up. For a second I wondered if she'd seen my run, and my pass, and then I wondered if she'd spoken to Auntie Mill about going round that day.

But then I stopped wondering all that because I could see what Daisy meant. And my insides froze, as if someone had poured a bag of dirty ice right down my throat.

Mum was standing next to a suitcase.

CHAPTER TWENTY-FOUR

But what's so bad about a suitcase?

If you're thinking that – well, before Christmas, Mum got ill. I mean, really ill.

She had to go into hospital and she stayed in there for *ages*. I didn't think she'd ever come out. She took a suitcase with her and there she was now, standing there with the SAME one. And yesterday she'd been miserable. So I stared at her, wondering what was going on, until she held her hand up to her mouth.

'Oh no!' she said. 'Don't worry!'

I swallowed. 'So you're not . . . ?'

Mum took my hands, letting out a long breath as she crouched down to me. 'I didn't think you'd assume that. Stupid of me. But no. Look, love, I'm absolutely fine.'

'You didn't seem that fine yesterday.'

'I know. That was silly of me. But I am. I *promise*.'

I tried not to show my relief. 'So what, then?'

'Ah. Well. It's just . . .'

'*What?*'

'Stephan,' Mum said.

I didn't understand what she could mean by that and I frowned. When she glanced down at the suitcase my eyes went wide.

'In *there*?' I cried.

'No!' Mum raised her eyes. 'Look, it all went a bit wrong at Auntie Mill's on Thursday, didn't it?'

'You could say that.'

'And I thought –' Mum glanced left and right – 'that he didn't like me any more.'

'Because you kicked food in his face?'

'And the rest.'

'But he does?'

'Well, he called me this morning.'

'And he still wants to get to know you better?'

'Yes. And so he's . . .'

'What?'

'Well, he's booked us some tickets.'

'For Charlton?!'

'Not *exactly*.'

'To what, then?'

'Paris,' Mum said.

'Paris!' I stared at her, panic rising inside me as I thought of Veronique. 'But I can't!' I cried. 'I need to be *here*.'

'It's all right,' Mum said. 'Calm down. He wasn't . . . Look, it's a shame you can't come, but I said you probably wouldn't be able to.'

'Thanks. But then why have you got the suitcase?'

'Ah.' Mum took a breath. 'Well, I thought, and only if it's okay with you, that *I*'d go on my own with him.'

'To Paris? For the day?'

'Two days. Stephan's girls are going to his mum's.'

'But won't the films all be in French?'

'We'll manage.'

'So . . . am I going to stay with Dad, then?'

Mum sighed at this, and I didn't know how I wanted her to answer. I don't know my dad that well. He didn't show up in my life until recently and I only see him every other weekend. Not even then sometimes, because he's an actor and he travels for work. I *did* want to see him but he lives in North London and that's *miles* away.

'He's touring,' Mum said. 'And Uncle Bill's away. Lance is too. And Mill's not answering. She's probably still in bed.'

'So?'

'You're coming home with us,' said a voice from behind me.

And when I turned round I simply could NOT believe who'd spoken to me.

Seeing Veronique and her mum at football was weird enough – Veronique *should* have been at her piano lesson. She had her exam soon. But – weirder – her mum was smiling. If *I*'d been sent to the head teacher, my mum would have stayed mad for about a year, but Veronique's mum didn't even look *angry*. So Veronique *wasn't* grounded? And even if she wasn't, weren't they too worried about Nanai to think about looking after me?

I was confused – but there was no way I was going to argue. This was GREAT! I'd tell Veronique about the CCTV. Then we could *both* confront Nanai. So I nodded, watching as Mum handed over my night bag to Veronique's mum, talking about when she'd be back. I thanked our coaches and then glanced over at Daisy, whose dad was jogging towards her. She had a ball at her feet, which he tried to nip off her, but she did a back-heel to Vi, who did a rabona to Lizzie, who 360-ed it back to Daisy, who did an L-sign at her dad and cracked up.

'Oh, look,' Mum said. 'The bus!'

Turning away from Daisy, I walked Mum down to the bus stop, where the 386 was about to move off. Mum piled on and then waved, me waving back until the bus was driving up towards Greenwich Park. Then I turned towards Veronique, who was walking towards me with her mum. I was *itching* to talk to her, wondering if I could do so with her mum there. But Veronique looked odd. She wasn't pale any more. She didn't look lost or worried, like she had at school. She didn't even look particularly serious like she normally does, as if she's thinking about some hard sum or something.

Veronique was *grinning*.

'It's Nanai!' she exclaimed, without me even having to ask. 'She's started to eat again!'

CHAPTER TWENTY-FIVE

Now *that* was surprising news. It was wonderful news. Brilliant news! The best news ever! Though it was also weird and, I'm ashamed to say, a bit disappointing. I'd been *so* focused on Nanai, I'd found stuff out that might help her and I was proud of that, actually. But it wasn't needed. I knew it was a stupid feeling, though, so I just said, 'Great!' and asked when it had happened.

'This morning. Fantastic, isn't it?'

I said yes but it still felt weird. And not quite real. And I thought about Mum, who'd be so disappointed when she found out: I could have gone to Paris with her after all!

I thought about getting Veronique's mum to phone Mum but the 386 was already out of sight. It was probably too late now and, anyway, there was another question that I wanted answering. So I just shrugged and followed Veronique and her mum through Blackheath until her mum stopped outside the fruit shop to chat to a friend.

'Wasn't she angry?' I whispered.

Veronique frowned. 'About what?'

'Marcus, of course.'

'Oh.' Veronique nodded. 'She went Vesuvius. I thought the roof would come off Mr Baker's office.'

'Blimey. But . . .'

'Yes?'

'Then how come I'm allowed over?'

'What? She wasn't angry with *me*.'

I stared at her. 'She wasn't?'

'No! She's complained about Marcus loads, how he picks on me. But they've never done *anything*. Mr Baker started telling her how my behaviour wasn't acceptable but she nearly tore his head off. In fact, I think she's finally decided . . .'

'What?'

Veronique's mouth opened but she stopped herself saying whatever it was. 'Never mind,' she mumbled, just as her mum said goodbye to her friend.

We went on again to their house, which is ten minutes beyond the village itself. When we got there, I saw just what it was that had tempted Nanai to eat again.

Veronique's dad was in their kitchen, which is smaller than Auntie Mill's kitchen next door because they've left it how it was and haven't knocked loads of walls down and stuff. It's nicer, though, because, whereas Auntie Mill's kitchen is so shiny that it can really hurt your eyes, Veronique's is old, and lived in, with drawers that don't quite shut and some of Veronique's art still on the fridge from when she was three. It always smells great too, though that morning it wasn't because of anything they'd made.

See, Veronique's mum's French. Because of that, her dad had gone to the French bakery in Blackheath for croissants – to welcome her home from her music tour. Veronique had taken two down to Nanai – and Nanai had eaten them. I said 'Great!' again, though the relief they were all feeling was still a bit weird to me. And when Veronique offered me one of the croissants I was suspicious – I couldn't see *why* they'd tempted Nanai. They didn't even have chocolate in. But then I tasted one and they were amazing! They weren't cardboardy like the ones Mum sometimes gets, but all buttery, and so flaky that my plate looked like a pile of autumn leaves when I'd finished. Kit-Kat was clearly a fan too because he tried to leap up on to my plate. Veronique grabbed him.

'They're his total favourite, aren't they, little rat-rat? But they're too rich. They're really bad for you, aren't they?'

She put Kit-Kat on the floor and gave him some peas instead. Then she took two more croissants down on a plate for Nanai. When she came back she turned to me.

'What shall we do?' she said.

Now, this was an interesting question. And it meant, of course, that I was having a playdate with a girl. None of the boys in my class would have asked me this because, in spite of the fact that we'd just been playing football all morning, we would obviously have gone outside to play football. I was glad she'd asked, though: with Nanai eating again we could go back to the other problem.

'We need to think about Mrs Martin,' I said.

First we discussed the JE (jelly event). Veronique made the point that blue jelly is actually quite unusual.

'So look for it at school,' she said.

Then we analysed the EB (exploding bag). We wrote down everything we could possibly think of on a piece of paper – but nothing came to us. Eventually we gave up.

'We just have to be vigilant,' Veronique insisted, 'in case the culprit re-offends.'

'Yes,' I agreed. '*And* we have to keep our eyes open in case the person who's doing it does it again.'

'That's what I just said.'

'Is it? Fantastic. Then we agree.'

'I wonder how she's feeling,' said Veronique, and I had an image of Mrs Martin at home all weekend, possibly in the giant Gruffalo onesie she wears on World Book Day. Just sitting there, wondering if she ever wanted to go back to a place where such horrible things were done to her. Something I haven't said is that Mum told me once that Mrs Martin has only EVER worked at St Saviour's. It must feel like her home.

'Is there nothing we can do?' I wondered.

'Actually,' Veronique said, 'there is.'

Veronique told me about *her* Person Project. Her scientist often took long walks, she said, to take his mind off a problem. Not thinking about it apparently gave him the answer. This had never once worked with my homework but I said okay, though a walk was out – the cloud buffaloes had stuck themselves together and it was raining. We played Pick-up Sticks instead, the pile making me think of Nanai's face.

'What now?' I said.

'We could play Scrabble,' Veronique suggested.

'Yes, or we could shoot ourselves instead. How about that?'

'What?' Veronique was astonished. 'Don't you *like* Scrabble?'

'Do *you*? It's a TOTAL snore-fest. Words? Spelling? We might as well be at school.'

'Don't you like school?' she said, equally astonished.

I didn't answer that. There was no point. Veronique is . . . well Veronique is Veronique. But I sighed. I was of course bound to get SMASHED if we played Scrabble, but Veronique *had* played Subbuteo at my house, hadn't she?

So – with a huge internal groan – I agreed. Veronique ran off to get the box like someone who's heard an ice-cream van, while I sighed. She put the box on the kitchen table and got the board out while I grabbed the letter bag. I drew a B. She drew an M. That meant I went first, so I shoved my hand back in the bag, trying to feel around for the blank ones. I didn't get any, though, and so I sighed again. Then, preparing myself for TOTAL humiliation, I set my letters down on the plastic rest.

And stared at them.

And I stared at them again.

And stared at them.

And stared at them.

And stared at them.

And then I stared at them.

And stared at them.

And stared at them.

And stared at them.

And then I stared at them.

And stared at them.

And stared at them.

And stared at them.

And then I stared at them.

And stared at them.

And stared at them.

And stared at them.

And then I stared at them.

And stared at them.

And stared at them.

And stared at them.

And then I stared at them.

And stared at them.

And stared at them until Veronique *hissed*. I didn't mean to be slow! But the best I'd come up with was 'AT'! I couldn't put that, though! It was TOO RUBBISH even for me! I stared *again*, and then I stared AGAIN as Veronique started to jiffle, moving her head from side to side in a way that was REALLY annoying. And I saw 'TEN'. Yes! That was a bit more like it and even though it was still pretty hopeless I decided to put it down.

But I stopped.

A miracle!

A word leapt into my head. It did it without *any* warning, as if a frog had simply hopped into my brain! What's more, it used ALL my letters! All SEVEN of them. Here they are again:

A E L Y N P T

See if you can get it too.

GO ON!

P E N A L T Y

Did you get it?

Well, I did, and it got me twenty-four on a double-word score, *plus* another twenty-four for using all my letters!

'Forty-eight!' I shouted.

'Right,' Veronique said. 'Well done. I suppose. Though can you be quicker next time?'

I said I would be, and Veronique had her go, getting a word I didn't even know. Then it was my turn again, and again I sighed, assuming that the first go was a fluke. But just like last time, another word frog jumped into my head! I got the following letters and added them to the A in PENALTY.

O R R C B S S

What do you think I got?

No – don't turn over until you've got it!

Yes –

C R O S S B A R

This was on another double-word score and got me forty-eight again! Veronique said 'Well done' again, though she sort of hissed it this time (she'd only got twelve points, and then fifteen). After that she tried to keep up with me but she didn't stand a chance because then I got HEADER, TACKLE, OFFSIDE, FULLBACK, HANDBALL, STEPOVER, STRIKER, DRIBBLING and PASSING, all of which used all my letters and totally piled on the points. Veronique kept *glaring* at me, which was weird because Scrabble's only a game, isn't it? And when I got my final word she absolutely fumed. The bag was empty and I only had six letters left (C, E, L, O, N and A), which I added to something Veronique had already put down.

'YES!' I said.

'You can't HAVE that!' Veronique yelled.

'Why not?'

'BARCELONA?'

'What's wrong with it?'

'It's a proper noun!'

'Well, if it's proper, I CAN have it, can't I? Anyway, most of *your* words I've never even heard of. You probably made them up.'

Veronique tried to argue but she was just being a bad loser. BARCELONA was on a triple-letter score and I got double for going out.

'Seventy-eight!' I bellowed. '*And* you have to take some points off for having letters left. That means . . .' I looked at Veronique, but suddenly she so wasn't so keen on doing a maths problem. 'I win by . . . *two hundred and sixty-one* points!!'

I couldn't *wait* to tell Miss Phillips.

CHAPTER TWENTY-SIX

Veronique jammed all the letters back in the bag while I did a worm celebration on the floor. She wanted a rematch but I didn't want to destroy her again. And we'd only played to give our minds a rest from thinking about Mrs Martin.

'Anything come to you yet?' I asked.

Veronique shook her head so I said we should distract ourselves some more by playing football. So we did, using the ball I bought her for Christmas (and which STILL looked suspiciously clean). I taught her how to side-foot it and not just do toe-prods. To encourage her, I told her again that Vi, Frieda and Daisy played.

'I know! I saw them earlier. They're excellent, aren't they? Lizzie's fab too.'

Wonderful.

After that Veronique did something weird. Get this – she suggested that we do our homework! I will repeat that. Veronique (NOT her mum or her dad) suggested that we voluntarily went inside, got out our schoolbags, and did our homework! When I answered that I didn't have my folder, Veronique told me that Mum had said it was in my bag. Upstairs in her room I saw that she was right and I sighed – until I thought of something. I could do my homework with *Veronique*! I slapped my folder down on her *really tidy* desk.

'Oh no,' she said. 'I think you'd better go on the floor. I mean, what if you saw mine by mistake? Or I saw yours? You wouldn't want us to accidentally cheat, would you?'

'No,' I said, 'of course not.'

Three minutes later I was on the floor looking at grammar problems. These were hard enough – but Kit-Kat wanted to play! He started nibbling my sheet till I pushed him off, and then I stared at the first sentence: 'The twins came in and asked if they could borrow Jennys crayons.'

We were doing apostrophes. I was supposed to put one in in the right place. This one seemed easy, actually – the apostrophe clearly went before the S in 'twins'. But when I went to put it in, Kit-Kat bit my finger. He bit it again when I went to put it just before the S in 'crayons'. The only place left was before the S in 'Jennys', which I was sure was wrong, though I put it in anyway to avoid being bitten again. And we did the whole test like that: me getting them right but Kit-Kat biting me so that I put them in the wrong place. When I'd finished, Veronique was still going.

'Done the apostrophes?'

'Miss Phillips didn't give me those.'

'Lucky! What did you get?'

'Semicolons.'

'I see. And if you get those right, will she give you some whole ones to do?'

'Oh, Cymbeline,' Veronique said, though it was to herself more than to me.

When Veronique had finished, she didn't just push her book aside but actually put it away in her schoolbag, before giving herself a tick on this planner thing on her wall. In one square I read 'Sleepover at Cymbeline's' while in another one was 'Cymbeline Staying'. The one for tomorrow said 'C.N.Y.'

'What's that?' I said, but Veronique shook her head

and told me to wait and see. Then we went downstairs again, which was when the whole day began to unravel.

Veronique's dad was coming in from the garden and he saw the Scrabble board.

'Fancy a game?' he asked Veronique's mum.

'Okay,' she replied. 'Prepare to die. I'll just do the washing-up.'

'Oh no,' I said, 'I'll do *that*, Mrs Chang.'

Now, the reason I was offering this was not because I had suddenly developed a *bizarre* fondness for washing up. During my life at home I have never once offered to do it, a policy I intend to stick to until I leave home (for my mansion, when I play for Charlton). But Mum goes ON about how I should behave at OTHER PEOPLE'S HOUSES, wanting to make other parents think that she's brought up a son who is helpful, tidy and polite. Instead of me. And it's not just her. You should see Lance. At his house he shoves his old pants down the side of his bed because he can't be bothered to go through to the washing basket. When his mum asked him to clear the table once, he actually started crying. But at our house he's so busy *offering* that we hardly get to *do* anything. It can't be long before parents work out the obvious: if they swapped all the kids round, permanently, their lives would be SO much easier.

Anyway, after *pretending* to be helpful so Mum would get told that I *was* helpful, Veronique's mum handed me this brush thing (which I presumed had something to do with the whole washing-up process). I took it over to the sink, where I was *fairly* sure washing-up happens. But I stopped. I took in the icebergs of foam waiting in the sink and the dirty dishes on the side. The coffee pot, the milk jug, a butter dish. And the plates. And I swallowed.

'Veronique,' I said, trying to keep my voice normal, 'can you go and get Nanai's other plate, please, so I can do them all?'

Veronique skipped out the French windows and I watched her go down to Nanai's cabin. But I didn't feel like skipping. I felt doubtful, nervous even. To take my mind off what I was thinking, I walked over to the table where Veronique's mum was staring at her first set of letters. She put a pretty good word down and then it was Veronique's dad's go. With a reluctant sigh he put FIELD down until I pointed at his three remaining letters.

'No,' I said, *MID*FIELD.'

'Isn't that two words?' objected Mrs Chang. Her husband went to get a dictionary – and then punched the air.

'One word! YES! Twenty-one, including double-letter scores, then a double-word score, then double because I used all my letters!'

'*Show me.*'

'Eighty-four!' her dad exclaimed, high-fiving me as Veronique's mum flicked through the dictionary to make sure he wasn't cheating, after which she gave me the same sort of glare Veronique had done earlier. Scrabble: these people certainly took it seriously.

Veronique ran up the garden with Nanai's plate and another huge grin on her face.

'Ta-dah!' she said, holding up the empty plate. And she wiggled her index finger at me: Nanai had nibbled it again!

Veronique handed me the plate and chatted about Nanai, how much she said she'd LOVED the croissants. But I walked over to the sink. I wasn't grinning. Not at all. I was more than doubtful now, I *was* nervous. And more than nervous: I was scared. My hands shook as I turned to the dirty dishes. The coffee pot and milk jug, and the butter dish. And then the plates. There were six of them. Four were from us: Veronique, her mum, her dad, and me. They were all covered in croissant flakes, a few white lines across one where I'd licked my finger and picked some up. But the other two plates, Nanai's plates, weren't like this.

Veronique and her parents were still talking about Nanai, how relieved they all were that she was eating again, what an awful scare it had been.

'How are you getting on, Cymbeline?'

'Fine,' I said, my back to them, as I turned to the last two plates. Nanai's plates. Which were clean. *Completely* clean.

They had no flakes on them at all.

CHAPTER TWENTY-SEVEN

That night I slept in Veronique's room on a trundle bed. After her mum put the lights out, Veronique chatted about Nanai, wondering if she'd eat other stuff now too. I didn't answer. I'd spent days wondering why she'd stopped. Veronique went on again about how great it was, but I didn't say anything. I thought about Daisy's dad. I still hadn't told Veronique about him – and I wasn't going to. Not now. Veronique was SO happy, while I just kept seeing Nanai's plates.

You're being stupid, I told myself. *It doesn't mean anything.*

But did it?

'Thanks for helping,' Veronique said with a yawn. 'It was really nice of you. We can go back to figuring out who's being horrible to Mrs Martin now. Daisy'll be pleased, won't she?'

I gave a mumbled yes but didn't say anything else. I just waited, and soon Veronique stopped moving. Then her breathing levelled out. I kept waiting. I stared at the ceiling, trying not to think the thoughts I was having, missing Mum, wishing I could talk to her about them. Thinking of Mum made me sleepy, though, so I shook my head and occupied myself trying to work out what I'd get if – somehow – I managed to get JACKYCHAPMAN on a triple-word score.

Then the door opened a crack.

'Night, kids,' whispered Veronique's mum.

I didn't reply, of course, and the door shut. Floorboards creaked. A tap ran. Another tap. A toilet flushed. The silence that followed wasn't really silence because I could hear cars sometimes and a dog barking. A police siren. But all these noises were coming from outside the house, so when I was *certain* that nothing was coming from *inside*, I pushed aside my duvet. I stood up, about to tiptoe to the door, when there was a scuffling sound from the corner.

'*Kit-Kat*,' I whispered, '*go back to sleep*.'

Kit-Kat wouldn't, though. He kept rattling the bars

of his box, obviously thinking I was getting up to play with him. Or do more grammar. Again I told him to be quiet, but Veronique was rolling over in her sleep. She started mumbling and was about to sit up. I managed to shush her back down again, desperate for Kit-Kat to quieten down until I realised that he wouldn't.

'Come *on*, then,' I whispered, opening his box and putting him on my shoulder. 'But behave yourself, okay?'

Kit-Kat gave my ear a nibble, which I took to mean yes.

It was dark in Veronique's bedroom and when I opened the door on to the landing it was even darker. I could barely see anything so I bent down to the bag Mum had packed for me. I don't like sleeping in the dark. I take my ghostie on sleepovers in case I wake up. I pulled it out, let Kit-Kat sniff it because he was curious, and took it out of the room. I turned it on and saw the stairs ahead of me, clicking it straight off again in case the light went up the next flight to Veronique's parents' room. Veronique's house is big but once I'd seen where the stairs were I knew I could find my way. Not that *that* helped me to calm down.

What AM I doing?

Trying not to think about it, I approached the stairs, though I didn't walk down them because I knew they were really squeaky. I slid down the bannisters instead, dismounted, then walked into the kitchen. There was a bit more light in there but not much so I clicked the ghostie on again and stared at the cupboards. I was fairly sure the key was in the end one – and I was right. I had to get a chair to reach up to the hook but I did that and took the set over to the French windows, where I asked myself again, *Am I really going to do this?* What if someone woke up and caught me? What would I say? There was nothing I could say, and I nearly turned round, thinking perhaps I could just talk to Veronique's mum and dad in the morning. But no. They were just as happy about Nanai eating again as Veronique.

I had to be certain.

I found the right key on the ring and opened the French windows, a blast of cold air coming in that made me wish I'd borrowed Veronique's dressing gown. I couldn't go back for it, though, so I stepped out on to the freezing patio. Up ahead, I could just make out Nanai's cabin, a ghostly black square in the darkness. I shut the door behind me and clicked off the ghostie, not wanting anyone to see it if they looked out of one of the windows. I sent my feet across the patio towards the grass, which wasn't so cold but was damp, weird beneath my naked feet. Wanting to get it over with, I walked quickly, though I nearly gasped out loud when my left foot connected with Veronique's football. It streaked ahead of me until it hit something – small and round which I might not have noticed otherwise. A quick click on of the ghostie showed me that it was a hedgehog, something I'd never seen before, something that was thrilling for a second until I stopped – Kit-Kat was scrabbling around at the back of my neck. He was panicking and I didn't know why, until I looked up and saw the black silhouette of a HUGE fox on top of Nanai's cabin!

I was terrified, but the fox hurried to the edge, looked over, and scurried down the side, disappearing into the bushes next to Auntie Mill's garden. I let out my breath and went forward again, keeping a lookout for any more hedgehogs.

When I got to Nanai's door I had a problem. There were other keys on the ring and I didn't know which was the right one. I got it eventually, though, and pushed the door open, hoping Nanai would be awake.

She slept so much during the day that I thought she might not be asleep now. And to begin with it seemed like I was right. Nanai has a little plug-in night light and in its glow I could see her – not in the small bed she has in there, but in her chair.

'Nanai,' I whispered, 'it's Cymbeline. Can I have a talk with you, please?'

No reply.

I sighed and stepped forward, peering down at Nanai. Her hands were folded on her lap, her glasses on a chain around her neck. Her eyes were closed. Once again I marvelled at how old she was, thinking it strange that she and I were both the same, were both people, because she looked so different from me. Getting to be Clay or Juni's age seemed a bit impossible, but to be *this* old? I shook my head, wanting to think about that but knowing I'd have to do it later. I wanted to wake her up. I wanted to ask her what was going on. But wouldn't she be terrified, suddenly finding me there? I sighed, knowing that I couldn't do it. And I realised that I didn't need to.

All I had to do was search the cabin.

For the croissants.

Kit-Kat jumped off my shoulder on to the back of

Nanai's chair. I watched as he sniffed her hair, and then stepped carefully down across the armrests before he leapt on to her footstool.

'*Stay there*,' I told him.

The first place I looked was in the bin next to Nanai, but I wasn't surprised when I found nothing. Nanai was too clever to put them in there – IF she'd only pretended to eat them. She'd know that someone would find them. A better place would be in one of her drawers and so, one by one, I opened them, feeling very uncomfortable about looking through her clothes. When I found nothing there, I knelt and looked under her bed as Kit-Kat just stood on Nanai's footstool, hopping up and down. He clearly wanted to play, but I sighed.

'You might want to help,' I told him.

I looked *everywhere*: the wardrobe, the little bathroom, under her chair, in a suitcase and in her handbag. I picked the photo of Nanai and her sister up from her side table, and the one of the big boat, which didn't have glass in the frame now. I even took the ghostie outside and looked at the back of the cabin in case she'd thrown her croissants out the window. But there was nothing.

I began to feel better. So I *was* being stupid. Nanai *had* eaten the croissants, *and* she'd scoffed all the flakes too! She must have *licked* the plates! She'd have been hungry enough. There were no croissants in the cabin because they were in Nanai! With intense relief I made my way back to Kit-Kat so that I could take him back inside.

But Kit-Kat wasn't having it.

Veronique's not-hamster simply refused to leave Nanai's footstool. When I tried to pick him up, he dug his claws into the fabric. I had to let go of him because if I hadn't he would have ripped it. I tried again but he clung on even tighter, and when I tried prising his paws off one by one he kept sticking them back on. Then he dodged round my hands. Really cross now, I tried to grab him again as he started scratching at something on the front edge of the footstool. I was terrified the sound might wake Nanai up – she's got a button by her chair that she can press for Veronique's mum and dad. What if they came running down there?!

'Kit-Kat,' I hissed, 'STOP IT!'

But then I saw what he was going for.

From the glow of Nanai's night light I could just

make out something metallic. Squinting hard I realised that it was a catch.

Nanai's footstool could *open*.

My heart sank, not least because Nanai's feet were on the stool. I'd have to lift them off. I did that – *CAREFULLY* – and then studied the stool, not wanting to open it. But Nanai was stirring and Kit-Kat was going CRAZY. He'd wake her up, I knew he would. So, without even thinking about it, I lifted the lid, watching as Kit-Kat dived inside.

On to the croissants.

There were four of them in there. Just as I'd thought. Seeing them was terrible. I pictured Veronique upstairs, how she'd wake up all happy. For a second I was SO angry with Nanai that I nearly woke her up to shout at her. But as Kit-Kat started gnawing at the nearest croissant, I stopped.

Because I'd seen what was underneath them.

CHAPTER TWENTY-EIGHT

I stared at the photograph which lay face down inside the footstool.

Kit-Kat was going bonkers, so I lifted him out, plus the four croissants that Nanai had pretended to eat. Then I turned my attention to the photo, clicking on my ghostie so I could see it properly. It wasn't in a frame, or an envelope (though Nanai might have thrown that away). It was small with some writing on the back, which, when I moved the ghostie closer, I could see was in Chinese. I had no idea what it meant of course so I turned the photo over, blinking at what I saw: Veronique. The photo was of her, holding a violin and smiling into the camera. I frowned. Was it just any old photo? No. Nanai had put it in her footstool with the croissants – where she obviously HID things. I'd never seen it before. Had Daisy's dad brought it to her? But if so, why? And who gave it to him? Couldn't they just have posted it? I had no way of knowing, so I turned the photo back over again so that I could see the writing, then I looked on Nanai's side table, where her Sudoku book was lying with a pen, next to her lamp and the framed photos.

I'd just finished copying the writing down on my wrist when my whole body went rigid.

Nanai was stirring.

I stared at her, staying completely still as she mumbled to herself some words that I couldn't understand. When she finally settled again, I let out a slow breath and turned to Kit-Kat, whose loud chomping was probably what had disturbed her. I took the croissants from him and shoved them back in the footstool. I put Kit-Kat back on my shoulder, peered out into the dark garden, and scampered back up to the house – quickly in case the fox was still there, only just managing to swerve round the hedgehog. Then I put the key back, shinned up the bannister (not easy) and slipped Kit-Kat back in his box.

Five minutes later I was asleep.

And it seemed like only five minutes after *that* that Veronique's voice shook me awake.

'Oh no!' I heard her complain.

I pushed myself up on to an elbow and blinked away what little sleep I'd had. Veronique was on the other side of the room. She was kneeling by Kit-Kat's box. I watched as she took him out.

'What is it?'

'He's all floppy!' Veronique lifted Kit-Kat up and inspected him. 'And look!'

'What?'

'Croissant crumbs!'

'Ah.'

'Mum!' Veronique exclaimed, before I could go on. 'She knows Kit-Kat shouldn't eat them but she can't resist him, can she, you naughty little rat-rat? It's his nose twitch, she falls for it every time. Well, that'll teach you, won't it?'

I climbed out of bed and went over as Veronique set Kit-Kat down in his straw, which he lay on looking green (if rats can look green). He looked as bad as I felt, actually, and I reached forward to scratch him underneath his chin.

'Thanks,' I mouthed, though I didn't know what I

had to thank him for. How on EARTH was I going I tell Veronique what I'd found last night? Not just proof that Nanai STILL WASN'T eating, but a strange new photo of HER, Veronique, hidden away in Nanai's footstool with Chinese writing on the back – which might just be the reason for everything!

The task of telling her was made harder when she stood up and then scampered over to the door. I followed her down to the kitchen in a daze, wanting the space to think about what I'd discovered. We were back at square one. We HAD to work out what was wrong with Nanai. Daisy's dad *must* have told her something, or brought that photo, but what did it mean? I wanted to discuss it with Veronique but she was distracted, buzzing about something. She slammed three cereal boxes down on the table and went to get some bowls.

'Don't have much, though,' she said.

'Why not?'

'Because we're going out for the best lunch you've ever had in your LIFE!' said her mum, as she came into the kitchen behind us.

I smiled at that and said, 'Great!' I wasn't really interested, though. I HAD to talk to Veronique, and do it (somehow) without upsetting her.

I was still trying to think of how I could do that when she went off to get dressed. Her mum said I should go and clean my teeth, which I did, though Mum hadn't put any toothpaste in for me and theirs tasted really wrong, like alien toothpaste might. And when I walked out the bathroom, something else was weird: Veronique's dad was wearing a suit and Veronique was in a posh dress, a shiny red Chinese one. Her mum was in one too (though she's French), while I stared down at my Charlton shirt.

'You're fine,' her dad said. 'Jacky Chapman fan? Seen his helicopter?'

'Yes,' I said, remembering that I was supposed to be doing my project on Nanai now. Well, I'd certainly found stuff out about *her*, hadn't I?

'Let's go!' said Veronique.

I still hadn't been able to get Veronique on her own to talk about the writing, and now we were all going out, though it was weird. They all thought things were okay, like they had been last night. But they weren't. And they were all obviously excited about wherever it was we were going, though Veronique wouldn't tell me where that was.

All the way to Blackheath station she chatted away, still SO excited about our morning and partly – I realised – because I was there. That should have made me feel great: I'd always wanted to be friends with Veronique and now we were: real friends. But I had a secret and I was keeping it from her. AND it was about her Nanai. It made me feel bad, cut off from her, and I wanted to get rid of it. But all I could do was sigh as Veronique chatted to her mum, asking if she'd remembered to tell her piano teacher that she wasn't coming that day.

We passed the Blackheath Music Centre place where Veronique does her piano lessons and crossed over towards the station. I thought we might get a bit of space alone there – but it didn't happen. We all sat together because the train was crowded. And it was strange. A lot of the people sitting near us were Chinese. And when the train stopped at Lewisham, more Chinese people got on, most of them in smart clothes. And then more got on at London Bridge. And when we pulled in to Charing Cross, there were THOUSANDS of Chinese people!

Charing Cross is in the middle of London. The street you come out on is called the Strand, which I know because Mum teaches art workshops at the National Gallery, across the road in Trafalgar Square. The Strand was PACKED and Trafalgar Square was HEAVING. That would have been pretty amazing on its own, but then I saw what was dancing through it.

'Look!' Veronique shouted, though I didn't need telling.

'What's happening?' I asked.

'It's Chinese New Year! Haven't you been before?'

I hadn't. I'd never even heard of it, though I didn't admit that. I just followed when Veronique's mum took her hand and led us into the square, jostled by all the people as we tried to get close to the dancing creature, which I could now see was a dragon.

Not a real dragon. It was a GIANT puppet, carried by about thirty people. It had huge white teeth in a mouth that was red and gold, little cymbals tinkling as it moved. The men carrying it wore gold trousers and blue waistcoats; some women at the front had super-white faces and these INCREDIBLE headdresses. Behind the dragon came a line of drummers, who seemed to be making the dragon dance. People took selfies and danced along too, waving red flags or little dragon puppets of their own.

'Well?' Veronique turned to flash me a smile. She was so thrilled and I could SO understand why. This whole thing was amazing, but it made me wince again. I just did my best to smile back as the dragon made its way to a big stage, set up between two of the Trafalgar Square lions.

There was music then, and dancing. We watched for a bit and then walked up past the National Gallery, where all the roads were shut. There was an EVEN BIGGER dragon in Leicester Square, after which my mouth literally dropped open. I'd been to the street that is Chinatown itself. But today it was hung with red paper lanterns, lots of smaller dragons dancing around beneath them to even more drummers, the sound SO loud as it thudded back off all the buildings. There were men with red-and-gold robes and long fake beards, their hats like snakes. Again I thought about trying to talk to Veronique but she kept pulling me off to see this thing, and that thing, before pointing to the end of the street. Another procession was marching towards us, this one of enormous inflatable pandas which went right over our heads. It was stunning and for a second it felt like I'd been whisked off to China.

But it wasn't *just* Chinese people. There were white

people and black people and Asian people. Outside one shop there were some very British-looking police officers with flags poking out from their uniforms. So we weren't in China: this was *my* city, where I live. *My* London. It made me feel bigger, as if there was more to me than I knew about. I looked at Veronique and felt something similar, remembering my thoughts when she'd first told me about Nanai. I'd thought that the Chinese bit of Veronique was, sort of, on the reverse side of her, that it had nothing to do with *me*. But if this party was here, where I lived, then that part of Veronique was connected to me too. It *wasn't* a bit of her that was different. Her Chinese bit was mixed in with her British bit. And if this was happening here, where I lived, then I was mixed in with it too.

In spite of what I'd found out last night (and how confused it had made me), I smiled. I couldn't help it – the colours and the noise swept me along. Soon, though, I began to get hungry and the thrill began to wane. I was nervous – Veronique had mentioned lunch and I didn't for ONE SECOND think she was talking about pizza.

She wasn't.

CHAPTER TWENTY-NINE

We watched some more dancers and listened to some singing, and then Veronique's mum said it was time for food.

'What are we going to have?' I asked, trying not to let the nerves show in my voice.

'Dim Sum.'

'What's that?' I asked Veronique, as we squeezed back the way we'd come. 'Sounds like something off CBeebies.'

'It's food.'

'What kind?'

Veronique told me to wait and see and so I sighed and just followed her through the crowd.

It wasn't long though before I found myself seated

in the noisiest restaurant I've ever been to (not that I've been to many restaurants). I was desperate to know what Dim Sum was, but when we got to the table there didn't seem to be any menus. I asked Veronique again but she wasn't listening, instead craning her neck, then pointing to a door at the back. A woman had come out. Through the forest of people I could see that she seemed to be pushing a wooden trolley, piled up with bamboo baskets. Veronique waved and the trolley edged towards us, after which Veronique started talking to the woman who was pushing it. Not in English. She spoke in Mandarin and I turned to her dad.

'Don't ask me,' he said with a shrug.

'What? Didn't Nanai teach you?'

Mr Chang shook his head. 'Nope. She wanted me to be English. Well, Veronique? What have we got?'

We all turned to Veronique as the trolley lady set a basket down before us. And Veronique grinned. '*Niu chang*,' she said. 'Want some?'

Veronique's mum and dad must have understood a little Mandarin because they both said yes. I kept silent as Veronique took the lid off the basket to reveal four white, slimy-looking roll things with steam rising up from them, which I stared at, trying not to remember Mum's rule about 'eating what is put in front of you'. In the past I've done this with cauliflower, celery, rice pudding and even artichokes, and I knew I was going to have to do it then. But after Veronique had put one of the rolls on her plate and poured this thin brown sauce on, she turned to me.

'Don't worry,' she said. 'There's lots of other stuff. That's the point of Dim Sum: you only have what you fancy.'

'Right,' I said, trying not to look relieved. 'I'll just, well, wait for the next one, then. Okay?'

Veronique said, 'Sure,' but it wasn't long before I was wishing that I'd had some of the *Niu chang*. Veronique and her parents slurped it down and then another trolley came along containing something Veronique called *Niu bai ye*.

'Yum,' I said. 'Though what *is* it?'

'Tripe.'

'Fantastic! Though what's *that*?'

'Stomach.'

'**STOMACH**?!'

'Better leave that one too, Cymbeline,' said Veronique's mum, reaching over to touch my arm.

'Not so keen on *Niu bai ye* myself.'

This time we *both* watched, as Veronique and her dad slurped the stomach down. What would the next trolley hold? Brain? Throat? The answer was even more surprising.

'Snowballs!' Veronique exclaimed, when she saw the baskets.

I frowned. The trolley lady put another basket down and when Veronique opened it I could see what she meant. At least – unlike the *Nia chang* and the *Niu bai ye* – the snowballs weren't slimy. I was staring at four white, doughy balls which I would HAVE to try. There was no way round it. With Veronique grinning at me, I picked up my fork and stabbed the nearest one before lifting it to my face. I sniffed it like Kit-Kat would have done – and relaxed. It didn't smell bad and when I nibbled it I was SO RELIEVED. It wasn't nice. It was dry and boring, like bread without the butter. I'd be able to finish it, though, and I nodded, matching Veronique who'd picked hers up in her fingers and really sunk her teeth in. But this gravy stuff splurged into my mouth! The snowball had something in it! I sat up, my eyes bolting open as I searched madly for a napkin – until I stopped again.

Because it was *THE* MOST delicious thing I have EVER tasted in my LIFE.

'I knew you'd like the snowballs!' Veronique laughed.

And I *did*. Veronique's mum and dad said they didn't mind, so I ate mine *and* the two left in the basket. They got another basket and I lifted the lid, knowing I could eat TEN. But I looked round the restaurant. Kids even younger than me were tucking in to all sorts of things. So was I something special?

'No,' I said, putting the lid down. 'Pass me the slimy things!'

And though I still liked the snowballs most, almost everything else WAS nice (not stomach). When I'd had enough, I was proud of myself. But as I looked around the table, a shadow passed over my mind. It was the secret I'd had since last night, the horrible secret. It had cut me off from the people around me. Then it was made worse – Veronique wrapped up two snowballs in some napkins.

'For Nanai!'

Veronique didn't know that Nanai wasn't going to eat them. How could I tell her? She was *so* happy. Could I tell her parents? But they were happy too, and it would mean I'd have to tell them about *how* I'd found the croissants. No. I wouldn't, not quite yet. I'd try to figure it out on my own first.

Very quickly I ran back through what I knew, my mind settling on Nanai, in her chair, looking angry at me, then throwing that photo across the room. Was it to do with that? I took a breath, then looked around the restaurant. There were other people, but most of the diners were Chinese. Like Nanai. I turned to Veronique's dad, who was drinking a small cup of tea.

'Mr Chang,' I said, 'do you think anyone else here was a refugee?'

Veronique's dad put his cup down. 'I don't know,' he said. 'Why?'

'I'm doing Nanai for a project,' I explained. 'I want to know what it was like on the boats when she escaped. But she won't say, will she?'

Mr Chang shook his head. Then he sighed. 'It's too hard for her. She's always wanted to live in the present.'

'But weren't you ever curious?'

He nodded. 'Of course. Asking Nanai was no use, though.'

'So?'

'So I found out in other ways.'

'Like a library or something?'

'Yes, but not only that. Come on,' he added, looking round for a waiter, 'I'll show you. It's just nearby.'

CHAPTER THIRTY

Veronique's dad looked around for a waiter. He paid the bill while Veronique just shrugged at me, clearly having no idea where we were going. Back outside we plunged into the busy streets again, though not for long. Round the corner was a café, the window brightly lit with amazing-looking dragon cakes, buns and rolls. I didn't think I could eat another bite – but it wasn't the food we were there for.

It was the walls.

The place was called Café Hoa. I stared at the sign and then at Mr Chang.

'The Hoa. They were the refugees,' I said, 'weren't they? The ones we called the boat people?'

Veronique's dad nodded, though he also explained

that not all the Hoa people left, and that some Vietnamese people left too. Then, when we'd squeezed our way into the busy café, he pointed at the walls – and I realised why he'd brought us here. They were covered in menus and prices, but they were *also* covered in photos.

Most of the photos were from newspapers. They were black and white, and they showed boats. The boats were crammed: people on the decks, or the sides, or clinging to the masts. Some of the boats were tilting, huge waves battering them, while others had sunk and were broken to pieces, debris spread all about. In one photo a boat was upside down, as if it had gone head over heels like the boat in the picture that Nanai had thrown. People were sitting on the upturned bottom, all dazed and exhausted while one man was screaming. In another one the people were piled so tightly on top of each other that I could hardly even *see* the boat. Other photos were worse. The next one wasn't of a boat but of a woman, in the sea, desperately trying to swim, though not to save herself. She was swimming towards three small children.

I stared at the photo and swallowed before pulling my eyes away, though the next one affected me even more. It showed another woman, not in the sea but on a beach. She was kneeling down and screaming and for a second I didn't know why. She was safe, wasn't she, kneeling on the sand? But in front of her was a bundle – just a bunch of rags, I thought – until I saw two tiny feet sticking out of the end.

I blinked at it.

Very quiet inside, I turned to Veronique, who was staring at the same picture, and we looked into each other's eyes for a second before Veronique shook her head. I knew what she was thinking because I was thinking it too: *this* was what being a refugee *meant*. Before then, we'd both known that Nanai had been one, but we didn't know that she'd gone through *this*. No wonder she didn't want to talk about it. I was stunned, amazed by Nanai, feeling stupid that I hadn't realised, stupid also for thinking it a bit odd that she wouldn't talk about it. How could she be normal and fun, and really kind, asking me about my football and stuff, when THIS had happened to her? *Weren't you always overwhelmed by it*, I wanted to say, *by the memories of what you'd seen? Especially if your sister hadn't made it.*

And then something else came to me: something I'd

seen on the news, about Libya and Italy, people trying to escape across the sea. But it couldn't be like this, could it? No one would let it be, not today, not knowing it had happened before. I turned to Veronique again, wondering if she'd know, but her eyes had shifted to the next wall.

This wall was different.

It still held photos. Most of the people in them, however, weren't in little boats. They were on bigger ships, on decks, or on land, and they didn't look terrified. Some were in queues. They were tired, but patient-looking. Not scared. In others they were even smiling. One showed a tall man in a British Navy uniform, shaking hands with a really happy-looking Chinese man. There were others like this, refugees standing next to other people who I think must have been their rescuers. In one frame there wasn't just a photo but a newspaper article with the headline 'WE'VE FOUND A HOME', and next to that was a big picture of a crowd of people looking cold and holding umbrellas, though they were still smiling. Were these refugees who'd been rescued? Who'd been given a new country to live in? Like ours? The answer must have been yes because the biggest picture there was a real photo, in colour, while the rest were in black and white. It showed a family, all huddled around a man wearing a Navy uniform, one man hugging him, the others smiling. And I suddenly realised something – it had been taken right where I was standing! Looking up at the counter, I saw that some of the people behind it were in the picture.

I shook my head and turned back to the first wall to see if I could spot any of those people who were *there*, in the photos of people on the boats or who'd been rescued. There were a few, I thought, but it was hard to be sure.

And then I looked for Nanai.

I searched for her amongst all the people clinging to masts or huddled together, and then I searched for her in the pictures of those who'd been brought here, to Britain. One woman did look a *bit* like her, but it was hard to see and she was holding a baby, anyway. I was scanning the rest of the photos when Veronique's dad appeared between us.

'Getting an idea?'

'Yes. Did Nanai really go through all *this*?'

He nodded.

'But how did she end up here?'

'A merchant ship picked her boat up and took her to Hong Kong. Some people wanted all the refugees sent back to Vietnam, but they'd have been killed. The British controlled Hong Kong in those days, and the British government eventually agreed to let some of the refugees live here.'

'Poor Nanai,' I said. 'It must have been really scary. Not just on the boats but later. Did she ever come here? To the Café Hoa, I mean?'

'I brought her here last year. I wanted her to open up a bit, but it was all a bit much for her. Especially these pictures, actually.' He pointed to the ones of the people who'd been rescued, the Navy people standing with them. 'She got really upset looking at those.'

'I bet,' said Veronique. 'Especially because . . .'

'What?'

'Well, she lost her sister, didn't she?'

'That's right.'

'And Nanai has never told you what happened to her?' I asked. 'To her sister, I mean?'

'No,' Veronique's dad said, and then he turned back to the wall that showed the smashed-up boats and the drowning people. My eyes fixed on a photo with no people in it at all. It just showed a wrecked boat surrounded by bags and suitcases and clothes, all floating in the sea. Veronique's dad sighed. 'But I think we know really, don't we?'

I was quiet then. So was Veronique. We didn't answer her dad's question. I just thought of the question Veronique had asked me after I'd gone down to see Nanai once: 'Don't you wish you had a sister?' Veronique did, but how much more did Nanai wish it? I was going to make that point to Veronique but, before I could, she went over to the counter and took a purse out of her bag. I turned back to the wall for one last look and my eyes fell on one of the pictures of the big ships, which looked like the one that Nanai had on her side table. The one she'd thrown. It looked a LOT like it, actually. In fact, wasn't that the EXACT same photograph?

Yes, I was sure of it. So was this the ship that had rescued her?

And had she seen it when she'd come here?

She could hardly have missed it, could she?

I stared at it and then turned again to the photos of the families, reunited with the captain who had saved them. Nanai must have seen these photos too. Something about that felt important, but I didn't know what. I was still pondering it all when Veronique came back from the counter. She had a thin cardboard box in her hand with four little cakes inside, shaped like fish.

'For Nanai,' she said.

I grew very quiet then, and I stayed quiet as we walked back down to Charing Cross. As we edged through the crowds, I had an odd vision: the streets all empty with nothing going on – because what would it be like if we *hadn't* helped those refugees? Would there be snowballs? Music and lanterns and dragons? I didn't know, but I was SO glad I lived in a country that welcomed people. It was like the pictures of the rescued people with the people who'd rescued them. They needed each other because without each other neither would have been able *be what they were.*

Nanai was SO lucky to have been rescued, but so was the person who'd rescued her. They were linked, like we were linked to Nanai. I decided that I'd say that to her. And I *would* tell Veronique about the croissants. It would be hard for her to know, but she had to – then we could *both* go down and demand the truth from Nanai. Why had that visit from Daisy's dad stopped her eating? What did that photo of Veronique mean, the one she'd put away in her footstool? I had to find out and there was only one way.

We *had* to ask her and we'd *make* her tell us. I promised myself that we'd do it AS SOON AS we were back at Veronique's.

But I *was* not expecting what happened before we got there.

CHAPTER THIRTY-ONE

I heard the laughing and the yelling when we turned into Veronique's road. It was coming from up ahead. Just some kids. A party probably. So what?

But then I realised *where* the sound was coming from.

Veronique's mum asked me if something was wrong. I shook my head. I just wanted to get past, to get into their house. But I couldn't.

'Hello, you two!' a voice said. 'You're a bit late! But never mind. Come on in, then!'

The woman who'd called out was standing by the road, saying goodbye to someone in a black BMW. The house she'd come out of was behind her and I glanced at the balloons on the door, tied together like a bunch of huge grapes. Then I turned back to the woman, who was now waving us over towards her.

Billy Lee's mum.

To realise that I had NOT been invited to Billy's birthday party stung. I've told you that he used to be the class super-horror but that we'd recently become friends. We *had*, and even though things had been weird with him recently, I'd been sort of pretending they weren't. I couldn't pretend now, though, and I wondered again how I'd upset him. Was it that own goal I scored against the Year 5s? It wasn't even my fault. It just flew in off my knee! I shook my head, telling myself I didn't care, as Billy's mum walked towards us, even posher-looking than Veronique's mum and dad. She had black high heels on that made her wobble a bit, and bright red lipstick. She said hello to Veronique's mum and dad, and then she smiled at Veronique.

'Don't you look lovely? What a nice party dress. If I could only get my Roxy into something like that.'

'Thanks,' Veronique said. 'But it's not a party dr—'

'Well, don't just stand there. Come on.' When we didn't move, she squinted at us. 'What is it, dears?'

'*Nothing*,' I said.

'Well, come on, then.'

'But we haven't been invited,' Veronique said.

Billy's mum frowned. 'Don't be *daft*, Veronique. I did the invites myself. I told Billy to put yours through your letterbox. He was to give you yours at school, Cymbeline.'

'Well . . .'

'You mean he *didn't*?'

'*No.*'

'He must have forgotten. Honestly. Kids!' She raised her eyes to Veronique's mum and then looked back at us. 'It's probably still in his bag. And yours'll be under your doormat, Veronique! But no matter. You're here now and that's the main thing. You've missed the pass the parcel but I've just got the ice cream out. Don't be shy, then!'

With that, Billy's mum took our wrists and literally pulled us towards the door, Veronique looking reluctant because she wouldn't want to go to Billy's party anyway, me no keener because, if I WASN'T invited, I didn't WANT to go – though I had at least missed the pass the parcel – which I HATE. The ONLY time I've EVER got the middle prize was at Juni's party (Year 3). It turned out to be a bright pink My Little

Pony that Juni was supposed to get, only Auntie Mill counted the layers wrong. Juni went BANANAS! And the last time I played was at Vi's, whose mum doesn't believe in presents in each layer. I made the mistake of sitting next to Daisy, whose arms are so long I never even TOUCHED the parcel. Lance won – a dinosaur puzzle that he stared at in amazement: his mum had donated it to the Autumn Fair two weeks earlier.

'In you go, then!' said Billy's mum.

She pushed the door open, the balloons bounced, and in we went. I tried to spot Billy, wanting to show him that I SO did not want to be at his *entirely pathetic* party. He wasn't in the living room, though, and he didn't seem to be on the bouncy castle, which I could see through the open patio door, Darren Cross on it with some kids I didn't know, probably from the Sunday football team Billy plays for. I had to admit it looked good, though, so I turned to Veronique, who shrugged. We walked towards it past the food table – or what was left of it. Two-and-a-half wrinkled mini-sausages sat abandoned on a foil tray next to an orange mountain. Advice to parents: just forget the carrot sticks.

I'd have a *little* bounce (I thought to myself). I wasn't going to whoop or anything, though. Then I'd get Veronique alone and, finally, I'd tell her about last night. With any luck we could simply avoid Billy, and perhaps even work out what was going on with Nanai. We walked through the kitchen and past Billy's present pile, a drone like Clay's on top. That sat next to the box for a MASSIVE Nerf gun, three footballs, some Scalextric track, a new Subbuteo team, a new Chelsea bag, a Chelsea scarf and a Chelsea shirt signed by the whole team (which reminded me that I *still* hadn't heard back from Jacky Chapman, which meant that I could probably forget about ever going in his helicopter). I tried not to gawp, remembering how Billy used to brag about how 'minted' his family was because his dad builds houses and flats. For a second I wondered what it would be like to get just about everything you ever wanted, plus some things you didn't even *know* you wanted. But Marcus Breen was leaning against the doorframe.

'Hey, Billy!' he called out, three Hula Hoops flying out of his mouth. 'I thought you said these losers weren't invited!!'

To hear Marcus say that was almost as bad as not being invited in the first place. I *like* Marcus, and I knew he was only saying that because of Billy. I nearly said something, but Marcus hadn't noticed that Billy's mum was right behind us. 'Marcus, *that*'s not very nice. And of course Veronique and Cymbeline were invited. Weren't they, Billy, love?'

For a second I thought that Billy's mum was crazy because Billy wasn't there. But then he walked through from a room on the left, his new Nerf gun in his hand. And he stopped, his mouth falling open in a way that told me that his mum was WRONG. He *was* surprised to see us. It wasn't a mistake. No way.

Billy hadn't invited us ON PURPOSE.

'Well?' his mum said, smiling at him.

Billy pulled himself together. 'Course they were. Yeah, I . . .'

'What?' I said.

'Well, I . . .'

'*What?*'

'Put your invite in your tray.'

'Did you? Really?'

'Yeah. Someone must have . . . I dunno. Doesn't matter, though, does it?'

'No,' said Billy's mum. 'They're here now anyway. But be more careful next time! How's the new gun?'

'Oh,' he said. 'Great.'

'Then why don't you give Cymbeline a go?'

'That's okay,' I said.

'Then what would you like to do, dear?'

'Er . . . we'll just go outside, won't we, Veronique?'

'Fine.'

'Okay, then. Billy, take Veronique and Cymbeline outside.'

'He doesn't have to take us,' I said.

'But I'm sure he wants to. Billy?'

Billy stared. '*Outside*?'

'That bouncy castle cost an arm and a leg and I think Cymbeline here's been eyeing it. Haven't you, dear?'

'Well . . .'

'Nah,' Billy said. 'I mean, why go outside, Cymbeline? It's cold.'

Billy's mum laughed. 'I know it's February but it's lovely weather. *Everyone*'s outside. The ice cream's out there.'

'I don't want any. Come on, Cymbeline, let's go up—'

'What?' Billy's mum frowned. 'You *asked* for it. I went to Asda *specially*. Raspberry ripple, you *insisted*.'

'Well, I've changed my mind.'

'Nonsense. Come *on*, you can see that Cymbeline

and Veronique want to go out, so off you go.'

But Billy didn't move.

'I'm not going.'

'*Billy?*' His mum narrowed her eyes. 'You're not—'

'Going out. I'm not. And . . .'

'What?'

'Neither are they.'

Billy's mum just stared at him and, I have to admit, we did too. 'Stop this nonsense. Your sister's out there serving the ice cream that YOU asked for. Off you go. *Now.*'

'No. And they're not going out either.'

'I *beg* your pardon?'

'This is my party, isn't it?'

'So?'

'Marcus was right. I *didn't* invite them. I don't want them here. Not in my house and not in my garden. And I definitely don't want them eating my ice cream! Tell them to leave!'

Billy stepped forward. He placed himself between us and the French windows as we just stood there. Dumbstruck. WAS it that own goal? But what had Veronique done? She clearly didn't know because she was looking at Billy like he was a disease, while Billy's mum glared at him, her voice like a tightrope as she said, 'Off you go, dears, while I deal with *this* young man.'

But Billy – who'd stepped in front of the door – didn't move. In fact, he tried to stop us. He jumped in our way until his mum flared, like a cobra, scowling at him as we edged past. Not that we wanted to. I didn't even want to go on the bouncy castle, which was now still, all the kids just staring at us.

'Go *on*, loves. We'll be out in a minute, **WON'T WE, BILLY?**'

With that, Billy's mum almost pushed us out on to the patio and slammed the door behind us! I glanced back in to see her round on Billy, towering over him, demanding to know what on *earth he thought he was playing at.*

'Not invited?' she said. 'What are you talking about?'

Billy argued, tears starting to stream down his face as Veronique and I stared. We were stunned. We could barely move because it was all so bizarre. Until Billy's sister said, 'Want some, then? Well? Can't stand here all day, can I?'

That seemed to break the spell and we both turned

away from the window. And saw Roxanne, leaning against a big wooden table with lots of old tiles stacked up behind it. She had her arms folded, two tubs of ice cream in front of her. Seeing her was a surprise: last time she'd been wearing lip gloss, white trainers, pink jeans and a Dua Lipa hoody. Now she was in black: black jeans, top, fingernails, hair, lipstick and nose ring (though she had a very white face). I thought she looked cool, though Halloween would be problem. It didn't leave her anywhere to go.

'Well?'

Veronique shook her head. 'I don't want any.'

'Suit yourself. What about you, then, Cymber-whatsit?'

'Oh.'

'It's not a difficult question. Do. You. Want. Some. Ice cream?'

I shrugged. I mean, I LOVE raspberry ripple normally but it was all *too odd*. We were at Billy's party which he didn't want us at, while he was getting shredded by his mum, the rest of the kids just staring at us. Roxanne must have taken my shrug for a yes, though, because she picked up a metal scoop with a sigh and dug it into the nearest tub. She pulled it out and flicked the ice cream on to a party plate.

'Anything with it?'

'Chocolate sauce?'

'Does this look like an ice cream van?'

'Sorry. This is fine.'

'No, it isn't!' screamed Veronique, from beside me. And before I could take the plate, Veronique grabbed it and thrust it back towards Roxanne! Then she pointed at something behind her. Huh? Had she gone mad too? I was about to insist that the ice cream WAS fine, and I reached out to take the plate.

But Roxanne had already turned round towards a bowl, which I hadn't been able to see because she'd been standing in front of it. And now I could see it. And it was big. Made of glass.

And brimful of something that made my mouth drop open.

As Roxanne dug the scoop into the jelly and held it over the ice cream, I glanced at Veronique. Her eyes were wide open. Then we both turned back to the French windows, where Billy was scrabbling to get out, actually fighting with his mum to pull the door open.

Then we turned to Roxanne again as she turned

the scoop over – and the jelly fell out on to the
ice cream.

CHAPTER THIRTY-TWO

The **BLUE** jelly.

CHAPTER THIRTY-THREE

Billy's mum dragged him up to his bedroom. But not before we'd met his eyes: and we could SEE. We could see that *he* knew that *we* knew why he hadn't wanted us to come outside.

We watched him go and then I ate the ice cream as fast as I could (*b-r-a-i-n f-r-e-e-z-e*). NOT the jelly. I took the plate inside, found a plastic bag near the present pile, and dropped it in.

'Should we show it to Daisy?' asked Veronique. 'Or just take it *straight* to Mr Baker?'

I didn't know, but one thing was certain – Veronique had been right before. Blue jelly isn't common *at all*. And when you combined it with Billy's weird behaviour? He'd said he HAD invited us until his mum suggested taking us outside – that was when he'd lost it.

Outside, where the jelly was.

I stared at it and then at Billy's present pile with all his Chelsea stuff – and I knew.

This was PROOF.

Proof he didn't want us to see.

'He *must* have come down from the heath,' I hissed, 'when no one was watching. Or maybe he did it *before* we even went up there.'

'Should we tell his mum?'

'Not sure.'

'After what he did?! And what if we don't tell and he does something else to Mrs Martin?'

'I *know*,' I said, but it still felt wrong to tell on him, especially as I had NO IDEA why he'd done it. Mrs Martin wasn't just great with the rest of us: she was great with Billy too. Miss Phillips gives him a hard time because he's not that academic, but Mrs Martin goes on about his sport all the time, really bigging him up. It was just too confusing, so I was glad when I didn't have to think about it any more: Veronique's mum came over to fetch us.

Mrs Chang was early – but we did NOT care. We were just so happy to get out of there and I was relieved to stop thinking about Billy. I could get down to the cabin, and Nanai. We weren't allowed to come away from Billy's without saying thank you, though. Veronique's mum called up the stairs and Billy's mum tottered down.

'Thanks for having us,' we said as Billy's mum did her best to look cheerful. There were tears in her eyes, though.

'Don't know what's got into him. All very embarrassing, I must say. But thanks for coming, you two.'

'We'll drop presents in another day,' said Mrs Chang, though I crossed my fingers behind my back. A present for Billy?

NO WAY.

We walked back past the present pile, Roxanne handing us party bags from a pile near the front door.

'Thanks,' I said.

'Oh, don't worry,' said Roxanne. 'Thanks for coming. It was such a thrill for me personally that you were able to take part in this celebration of the life of my younger brother. Seriously, I was deeply touched. Please shut the door behind you.'

I did that. And then, back in Veronique's kitchen, I

stood for a second, thinking about how I'd start things with Nanai, staring at their dish drainer where there were still six plates waiting to be put away. I'd ask her whether she'd hired Daisy's dad, and what he'd come to see her about, and whether it was him who'd brought her the photo of Veronique. I'd ask her why that had affected her so badly and what exactly she'd seen at Café Hoa that had upset her, when Veronique's dad had taken her there last year. I was about to ask if I could go and see her when Veronique turned to her mum.

'Why did you come so early? Is it so I can practise? My exam's on Saturday, isn't it?'

Her mum nodded.

'Then I really should be getting on with it.'

'Don't worry about that just now,' her mum said.

'It's not that?'

'No.' Veronique's mum shook her head. And then she sighed, and reached for Veronique's hand, Veronique frowning until suddenly she turned, and stared out of the French windows into the garden.

The cabin at the bottom was dark.

The door was wide open.

CHAPTER THIRTY-FOUR

When Veronique's mum told us that Nanai was back in hospital we just stared at her. I couldn't believe it. I *had* to speak to her. As for Veronique, she fought the idea as if it couldn't be true: not now that Nanai *was eating again*. But when she *had* accepted it, her bottom lip began to wobble.

'Well, this time I'm going too,' she said. 'And *nothing* is going to stop me.'

Mrs Chang thought about arguing but changed her mind. Although, there was a problem.

Me.

'But I'll be fine,' I insisted.

'Sorry, we can't leave you here on your own.'

'Kit-Kat can look after me.'

'That wouldn't be right, Cymbeline. Let's see where your mum is, shall we?'

Veronique's mum called my mum, who was on the Eurostar, about an hour outside London. Veronique's mum said we'd have to wait for her, but I shook my head.

'I want to see Nanai too!'

She eventually agreed and we hurried out to their car.

'Which hospital have they taken her to?' Veronique asked.

The answer was Lewisham Hospital. This might ring a bell in your head, actually, because it used to be on the news A LOT. When we were in Year 3 the government wanted to shut it down. People phoned up radio stations, wrote angry letters to the newspapers and put posters up in their windows. (Mum put two up in case one fell off.) Mrs Martin was in charge of it all because her sister is a nurse there. She organised meetings at the school, got T-shirts made, and handed out leaflets for people to put through doors. This was all because Lewisham Hospital is BRILLIANT.

On my first time there I went from *before* me to *actual* me (born). The second time was when Mum thought I had this thing called meningitis (very bad). I didn't, but if I *had* had it, any other hospital would have been too far away (so end of Cymbeline). Other times I actually remember include when I broke my arm falling off the Thomas the Tank Engine at Tesco (Lance's fault), when I broke my finger playing Cluedo (Marcus Breen's fault), and when I had to have a small piece of pink plastic removed from inside my left ear (My Little Pony leg, Juni's fault).

In all cases I was treated fantastically, something not unusual because everyone you speak to has similar stories of great nurses and fabulous doctors, so the whole campaign to keep it open culminated in this GIANT demonstration outside. This finally saved the hospital, which is something you can thank ME for.

See, Mum and I met other St Saviour's families at Lewisham station. Mrs Martin led us down the road, where we shouted REALLY loud, though that wasn't what did it. Mum got a bit overexcited with her 'Save Our Hospital' placard and she knocked me out with it.

'Look!' I could hear her shouting as I was regaining consciousness. She'd picked me up and was hurrying me into Accident and Emergency, followed by all these TV cameras. 'What would I do now if this hospital was closed? Where would I **GO**, hey?'

Later we were on the news!

'Well, Prime Minister,' the presenter said, after the film had ended, 'what can you say to that desperate mother? What *is* your answer to her?'

Next day they decided to keep the place open. And the next time I had to go to Lewisham Hospital (food poisoning, Auntie Mill's fault), everyone recognised me! The staff didn't even mind when I threw up on them!

I didn't want Nanai to be in hospital, but if she had to be in one, I was glad it was Lewisham. After we'd parked, we walked to the main door, where a nurse said, 'Hi, Cymbeline!' and pulled me inside. I was patted on the back by two receptionists, a porter, the lady who runs the flower stand, and three doctors, who all asked me what was wrong.

When I explained that we were actually there for Veronique's granny, the nurse led us to this massive lift. A porter pushed a bed inside with us. On it was a very old man, soft white hair floating down his stubbly, sunk-in face. He was curled up like a baby, his eyes closed, and he looked distressed by the plastic tube going into the top of his hand. He was trying to get it out but a woman beside him stroked his hair.

'S'all right, Dad,' she said. Then she bent down and kissed his forehead.

When the lift pinged, we followed the bed down a corridor and into a ward. And saw more old people. *Really* old people. A large woman with no teeth was sleeping with her mouth open, staring up at the ceiling. Another woman dozed in a wheelchair, her head covered in dark spots like the skin of a giraffe. And then, before I was ready for it, a hand seemed to grasp my heart.

Because there was Nanai.

And she too looked old in a way I'd never thought of her before. We'd played football really recently, laughed and talked about Jacky Chapman's helicopter. Now she was lying asleep in a bed that was far too big for her, metal bars above her head, a tube in her hand like the man had had, wires coming up from her chest. Veronique stopped as if she'd been punched, while I just blinked, like I'd been shown backstage at a theatre and all the magic had suddenly vanished. Nanai couldn't pretend any more, she couldn't get herself together to appear all energetic.

She was just *there*.

I hadn't seen Veronique's dad. He was sitting next to the bed, but I didn't notice him until he stood up.

'Hello,' was all he said.

We sat down, me on a chair and Veronique on the side of the bed, holding the hand that didn't have a tube in. I didn't know what to do, so I did nothing, not even speaking, barely even daring to breathe. I didn't want to take any of the air that Nanai might need.

Silently I hoped that Mum would come, and then I hated myself for thinking that. Veronique's mum and dad chatted about the doctors, how they didn't know what was wrong yet, how they were waiting until Nanai woke up. I just looked at the sheet covering her as it kept going up a little, then down again, relieved every time it moved.

'Mum,' Veronique said, after what seemed like ages, 'is there a loo?'

Mrs Chang smiled and took her hand. They walked off and it was a bit of a relief for some reason. I shifted in my chair and smiled at Mr Chang – though my smile faded. He looked serious. He glanced after Veronique then pulled his backpack on to his knee.

'Cymbeline,' he said, 'I have something for you.'

'Oh? Really?'

'Yes,' he said.

And then he pulled out my ghostie.

For a second I didn't understand. And I stared at it. My night light? How did *he* have it? I frowned – but then it came to me. And I couldn't breathe. My face was burning and my throat was dry.

My secret night-time expedition.

CHAPTER THIRTY-FIVE

It wasn't so secret after all.

'Did I . . . ?' I stared at the ghostie.

'Yes?'

'. . . leave it in Nanai's cabin?'

Mr Chang nodded. 'I found it this morning when I went to check on her. I was going to tell you before, but I didn't want to do it in front of Veronique.'

'Oh,' I said, the word like a sharp stone as I forced it out of my throat. *How could I have been so stupid?* 'And did you . . . ?'

'Yes?'

'Find the croissants?'

He nodded. 'At least she ate a little bit.'

'She didn't,' I said. 'That was Kit-Kat.'

'Oh. He was your partner in crime, was he?'

The word 'crime' sent a hot wave of shame right through me. I was their *guest*. I'd gone wandering around in their house in the middle of the night – *and* I'd kept secrets from them.

'I'm so sorry, Mr Chang.'

'For . . . ?'

'Going down there. I . . .'

'Should have told us what you were suspecting?'

I nodded and Mr Chang sighed. 'Perhaps. But we were all so happy, weren't we? You were worried.'

'I thought you'd be upset. I needed to be sure I was right.'

'Well, you were. I was going to talk to Nanai about it when we got back.'

'But she was ill?'

'Yes.'

'I'm really sorry,' I said again, but Mr Chang smiled.

'You *needn't* be.'

What? 'Needn't I?'

'No.' He looked down the ward, the way that Veronique and her mum had gone. 'You care about our family. You care about Veronique. Were you scared?'

I had a flash of that huge fox, and nodded.

'Then I admire you, Cymbeline. Though if there's anything else you need to tell me, please do.'

I took a breath. 'Did you find the photo?'

'The . . . ?'

'In the footstool? Of Veronique?'

'Yes,' he said, 'but—'

'Have you ever seen that photo before, in Nanai's cabin?'

'Why?'

'It might be important. Please – have you?'

He frowned. 'No, as a matter of fact. I mean, I have; it was in our living room. But it was in a frame before, and it didn't have Chinese writing on it. We noticed it was gone from the sideboard but we thought it had fallen down behind something, or—'

I nodded. 'Nanai hired a private detective,' I said. 'I think he brought that photo to her. Or *back* to her,' I added, thinking of how it used to be in the living room. 'Last Sunday.'

The words were so shocking to Mr Chang that he just stared at me.

'A *private detective*?' he asked, eventually.

From the way he was grimacing I could tell he didn't believe me, so, quickly, I told him about seeing Daisy's dad on Auntie Mill's CCTV. He shook his head, stared at Nanai, and then back at me again.

'She must have given it to him and he brought it back,' I said. 'That photo. He must have. With some sort of message, I guess? And that's what stopped Nanai eating.'

'But *why*?' said Mr Chang, blinking hard and grimacing again, before he turned once more to Nanai, who was still very much asleep in her big metal bed.

When Nanai didn't answer, Mr Chang turned back to me, about to ask me again. But Veronique and her mum came back. And then *my* mum came, leaving her suitcase at the entrance to the ward before hurrying in towards us. She gave Mrs Chang a hug, hugged Veronique too, and sighed towards Mr Chang.

'If I'd known,' she said, 'really, I would never have . . .'

'That's all right. We had no idea either. And we've loved having Cymbeline.'

'Well, that's a relief. Was he good?'

'Mostly.' Veronique's mum turned to me, her face tightening as I swallowed. Did she know about my midnight trip too? But was she angry about that? 'You must never help my husband at Scrabble again,

Cymbeline. Okay?'

I sighed and said I wouldn't, and then it was time for Mum and me to go.

I thanked Veronique's mum and dad, especially for the lunch. And then I turned to Veronique. Who looked lost. Scared. Fragile, like she was made out of tissue paper. After a quick glance at Nanai, I walked down the ward and when I looked back Veronique gave me a smile that was hardly even there, staring across at me until Mum led me out into the corridor.

'She'll be all right.' Mum ruffled my hair but I shook her hand away, this huge sense of helplessness crawling all over me. I was useless. Veronique had wanted me to help her and I'd failed. I wanted to go back, to *do* something. But Mum took my hand and led me off to the lift where she told me that Mr Uber was going to take us home again.

But it wasn't him. It must have been his brother.

CHAPTER THIRTY-SIX

From Paris I got a drawing pad (normal size), a Toblerone (BIG) and an Eiffel Tower (small). Mum gave me them back at home – but they were nothing to me. I'd known that Nanai wasn't eating. Now she was ill again. *Really* ill. That fact came before everything. I wasn't even thrilled when Mum handed me a soft package that turned out to be a genuine PSG football shirt (the best team in France). It wasn't even from her. Mum told me it was actually from Stephan, which confused me. Why was he buying me something as expensive as this? Mum asked if I wanted to try it on but I said no and put it back in the bag.

'Thank him for me, though, won't you?'

'Wouldn't you like to thank him yourself?'

'No, you can do it.'

'Really? You could maybe take him to see Charlton if you like. They won yesterday – I checked. Didn't you know?'

'No. I didn't. And it's okay. Really. *You* can thank him.'

Mum's mouth opened to reply, but she changed her mind.

She took her suitcase up the stairs then, and I sat on her bed as she unpacked it. She sprayed some French perfume on and asked me what I'd been getting up to. I told her about Chinese New Year, the colours and the sounds all coming back to me as I went through it. They meant nothing to me now, though, either. They even sickened me because I thought of us there, enjoying it, while Nanai had been at home. Alone. Feeling so ill that when we got back she'd had to go into hospital.

Would it have been different if I'd said something in the morning about the croissants? I didn't know, and when Mum asked what I was thinking I told her about how Veronique had thought Nanai WAS eating. I didn't say how I knew she wasn't. Mum sighed and I stared at her, wanting so much for her to tell me not to worry, that *Nanai would soon get better*. But she didn't. Instead she pursed her lips, not knowing what to say. To change the subject she asked about the party.

'Billy's mum texted to apologise for something. Everything okay?'

I told her about the jelly. When she didn't get it, I was angry. I went back over what had been happening to Mrs Martin and it was like she was hearing it for the first time.

'I'm surprised there's been nothing about it from the school.'

I sighed and went to get the letter that had been in my bag for almost a week now. Mum must have realised how upset I was about Nanai, though, because she wasn't cross. She just opened it and squinted.

'That's weird.'

'It's terrible!'

'No – this isn't about Mrs Martin.' She stared at the letter. 'Something about developing stronger ties with other school chains and some changes to, let me see . . . "*statutory designated usage of the school buildings*".'

'What?'

'What indeed! They probably want to have more functions, to raise money. There's a governors' meeting on Saturday evening to approve it. Whatever "it" is.'

She shook her head and tossed the letter aside. It could stay there as far as I was concerned. I just wanted to think about Nanai.

'But this thing at school,' she said. '*Billy*'s doing it?'

'You should have seen how he tried to keep us inside.'

'Well, I don't want you causing trouble. Leave it to me. I'll mention it to Mr Baker. Don't say *anything* that'll get you into any fights, okay?'

I hissed out an 'okay', though one thing was certain: there was no way I was going to let Billy get away with it.

'What do you think?' Mum said, holding her left wrist in front of my face, the perfume biting into my nostrils. I grimaced.

'It doesn't smell like you,' I said.

We had supper then, but I couldn't eat. I HAD to come up with something I could do for Veronique. I COULDN'T let her down – because I knew what that felt like. Jacky Chapman wasn't going to get back to me. I knew that now. He wasn't going to take me to a game in his helicopter, and bring me home after. I'd told Miss Phillips that I didn't care – but I *did* care. I looked up to him. I thought he was special. And I didn't even know him! But I did know Veronique – she was my friend and I was GOING TO HELP HER.

And I had one chance left: I HAD to see Daisy. Her dad knew why he'd gone to see Nanai AND he knew what he'd taken her. I couldn't do that now, though, so I squeezed my mind for something else. Nothing came, so I went to clean my teeth – which was when I saw the Chinese writing on my wrist.

I got mum's phone and FaceTimed Veronique's mum, then asked to speak to Veronique.

'Nanai's still asleep,' she said.

'Oh.'

'But I'm not going until she wakes up. I'm staying here.'

'That's good. But . . .'

'Yes?'

I pointed the camera at my arm.

'What's that?'

'It's just something I saw. I wanted to know what it meant, so I copied it.'

'Oh. "Granddaughter".'

I moved the phone back to my face. 'As in "you"?'

'That's right.'

'I see,' I said, though I didn't. Why would Daisy's

dad bring Nanai back a picture of Veronique, with 'Granddaughter' written on the back? And why should it stop her eating?

In bed I stared at the ceiling. The darkness was all swimming and purple. *Daisy's dad. The photo of Veronique inside the footstool.* There was an answer to it. I *knew* there was. A simple answer like a word, hiding in a jumble of Scrabble letters.

Only this time the answer wouldn't come.

CHAPTER THIRTY-SEVEN

I found Daisy just inside the school gates. My last chance. Her stick of rock was down to the size of her hand now, and it seemed to symbolise everything. There was hardly any time left. Soon there would be nothing. I started to tell Daisy what I wanted, but she frowned at me.

'Why are you in school uniform?'

'What?'

'*Uniform*,' she said. And she opened her coat to reveal, not a St Saviour's jumper and trousers, but leggings. And a sweatshirt. And I groaned. Mum is ALWAYS forgetting Own Clothes Day. But Daisy sighed.

'*He-llo?* The tournament?'

'What?'

'The *athletics* tournament, dimbo!'

Of course! Daisy was talking about the reason we'd been doing running the day of the JE (jelly event). It was a try-out, to choose people to go to a joint Year 4 and 3 athletics match, and I'd been picked.

'That's today?' I asked.

'Yes! Go and get your kit on!'

'I will,' I said. 'But then you *have* to invite me for a playdate.'

'Tell *your* people to call *my* people.'

'No. *Today*.'

'But I've got ballet.'

'Not today you haven't. I've got something to *tell* you. About Mrs Martin.'

'SO TELL ME!'

'I can't,' I insisted, as Billy Lee ducked by, trying to hide behind some Year 5s. 'I'm not allowed. Not *here*. Go and ask!'

Daisy did, as I went upstairs to change, VERY relieved that I wasn't going to be the only kid in uniform – AGAIN. Lance and Danny Jones take bets, Match Attax changing hands when they see me. Even the Reception kids laugh, not pleasant unless you *like* being ridiculed by miniature Bob the Builders, Spider-men and unicorns. And Mum doesn't just forget Own Clothes Day. Last year she forgot World Book Day, and there were so many cloaks and wands in the playground that I felt like some normal kid who'd tripped through Platform 9¾ by mistake. Marcus Breen called me a muggle so many times I nearly punched him. Mum promised to make it up to me, so *this* year she spent ages making me what, I will admit, was a great costume. But when she sent me in – IT WASN'T WORLD BOOK DAY! That was the *next* week.

'Gandalf,' Miss Phillips kept saying, ALL day, 'you should know the answer to this one, being a wizard and all.'

I was annoyed now, though. I'd wanted to spend all day figuring out what to say to Daisy's dad. But what could I do? I ran back down – and stopped.

Mrs Martin was standing near the office.

To see Mrs Martin there was strange. I knew it WAS her, but she was different. Not bubbly. Not friendly. She looked stressed, sighing when she saw me and telling me to get a move on, snapping at one of the Year 3s who didn't have his bag. And the kids acted differently too, just standing quietly like she was a normal teacher instead of jumping round her, asking what events we'd be doing. When she asked if we all had our packed lunches, I nodded, not wanting to get told off.

'You can share mine,' Daisy whispered, as the Year 3 kid came back.

There were four Year 3s: strange because there were only three of us – Daisy, Billy and me. Vi had come fourth in the trial, so where was she?

'Ill,' Mrs Martin said. 'We're waiting for a replacement.'

Miss Phillips came out then – with Veronique. Veronique hadn't even been at the trial, though I could understand why they'd chosen her. Miss Phillips must have been told about Nanai. Perhaps they thought this would cheer her up though I didn't think it would.

'Is Nanai still in hospital?' I asked, as Veronique walked towards us. She nodded and looked down at her feet.

'Right,' said Mrs Martin. 'If we can all keep up, then we might just get this train.'

'Wait!' called a voice from behind her.

The voice belonged to Mr Baker. He'd come out of his office with his phone in his hand. There were disruptions, he said. And cancellations.

'Great,' Mrs Martin said. 'Just what we need.'

'Don't worry,' said Mr Baker. 'Got your car?'

'Yes, but there are *eight* of them.'

'I'll take half. I'll drop them off and pick them up later, yes? Come on, children,' he added, before Mrs Martin could reply.

We all hurried round to the staff car park. Mr Baker told us Year 4s to get in with him and I was relieved. I was still wary of Mrs Martin, still nervous about what she was thinking. I was also impressed by Mr Baker's car, which wasn't quite Auntie Mill standard but still had shiny leather seats and a great-looking satnav.

'Can I sit in the front?'

'Daisy, I think,' said Mr Baker. 'She's tallest.'

So I had to get in the back, climbing in after Veronique. Billy got in after me and I shuffled as far away from him as I could.

'Righto,' said Mr Baker, turning round to smile at us.

It was weird then. As Mr Baker pulled out of the car park and drove up through Blackheath Village, he kept asking us questions: who was good at what sport, whether we were looking forward to the Lewisham Cup. He chatted like someone's dad, which wasn't something I'd been expecting because normally he's so, well, separate. He was still our head teacher, though, which meant that we couldn't relax, something made worse because the traffic was bad and it took ages. It was a relief when we stopped at the venue and climbed out.

'Good luck!' Mr Baker called. 'Do your best!'

'Come on, then,' Mrs Martin said, locking up her little white Renault and shoving her keys in her bag.

We were at Sutcliffe Park. It's a real athletics club with a proper running track and a little grandstand for spectators. Inside they've even got a climbing wall and a skateboard track, which we saw through the windows as we walked round to the front, where there were LOADS of kids from LOADS of different schools, plus official-looking adults.

'St Saviour's?' said one, as he stared at his clipboard. 'You're late.'

'Yes,' Mrs Martin replied. 'The trains, they—'

The man wasn't listening. 'Most annoying when you're trying to run things. Nearly docked you some points. Who are your Year 3 sprinters?'

'Just a second,' Mrs Martin said, 'and very nice to see you too, I must say,' she muttered as she turned round to us.

We'd barely even got our breaths back and certainly hadn't had time to warm up. But there was nothing for it: three Year 3 sprinters were needed and one was needed straight away because the first Year 3 heat was about to start. Mrs Martin hurried Maeve Brennan to the track and I shouted out good luck. But Daisy punched my arm!

'What are you *doing*?'

'Hey!' I objected. 'What do you mean?'

'We don't want her to *win*,' Daisy said (like I was stupid).

'Don't we?'

'No! We have to do *better* than them.'

I looked at her. 'But they're from OUR school.'

'I know. But it doesn't matter if we lose to these other kids.' Daisy looked round dismissively. 'We'll never see them again. But if we don't do better than the Year 3s, they'll go on about it FOREVER.'

'Right,' I said, as Maeve walked up to the start line. And I soon saw what Daisy meant. Maeve won her heat and the other Year 3s went crazy.

'EAT THAT!' the littlest one said, when Mrs Martin wasn't looking.

And then it was war. There were more Year 3 sprint heats but fortunately the St Saviour's boy in the next one came last. In the next one the St Saviour's girl did something really stupid: she stopped to help another kid who'd fallen over!

'SUCKER!' shouted Daisy, as Mrs Martin urged the girl to carry on. She still managed to come third, but it could have been worse.

'We'll nail it!' Daisy said.

'Year 4 sprints!' shouted one of the organisers.

We were a bit more prepared now. Mrs Martin turned to Billy Lee, the rest of the kids approaching the starting line. By now I could see the way the competition was organised. The fastest kids from each school were matched against the fastest kids in other schools. Lining up were some really fit-looking kids, one doing these professional stretches, turning his trainers up to show spikes underneath.

'He reckons it's the Olympics,' Daisy said, which made me think of Mrs Martin. She really wasn't her usual self. She was wary, keeping a sort of distance from us, which wasn't physical but which I could really feel. Perhaps, if we won, it would change that, and I turned to Billy, prepared to actually cheer him on.

But he just stood there.

'Billy? Come on, then,' said Mrs Martin.

He bit his lip. 'I'm not feeling very well.'

'*Really?*'

'Yes. Really.'

'Well, you could have said back at school!'

'It's only just started.'

'Has it? Blimey. Well, just do your best.'

'I can't, miss,' Billy said, still not moving, folding his arms and shaking his head while I glared at him. All right, he *didn't* look great, but it was just because he'd seen who he'd be up against. What a COWARD!

'St Saviour's!' the organiser called out, and Mrs Martin turned to Daisy.

'Me?' she said, pointing at herself.

The answer was yes. Daisy had to run in the Year 4 Heat 1. The Year 3s were high-fiving each other, but not for long. Daisy blushed, shrugged, and stepped forward. All the other kids went into these posy-looking crouches while she just stood there, something that didn't seem to change after the pistol was fired, until she realised that she should probably get moving. And she BLITZED it, coming from way behind to win. It meant that when I only came fourth in the heat that she was supposed to be in, it wasn't so bad.

It was Veronique's turn next, though she wasn't paying attention, just staring into space so that she didn't hear Mrs Martin call her name. She got herself together, though, and actually came second, a smile on her face afterwards in spite of what she must have been feeling.

It didn't last long. While we ate our snacks, she reached into her bag.

'Mum lent me her phone,' she explained. 'Dad said he'd text if there was any news.'

'And?'

Veronique showed me the phone and I saw there was nothing on it. She shoved it back in and wandered off to the loo. I stared after her until something happened.

And it was something that gave me a clue about Nanai.

CHAPTER THIRTY-EIGHT

A teacher from another school came over and said she was looking for one of her kids. While Mrs Martin pointed off towards the loos, where the kid had probably gone, I blinked at her.

She was *looking for someone*.

Daisy's dad did that. Not often, he said, but now and then. I remembered his words from the heath: '*Sometimes, finding people is actually worse, believe it or not. Worse than if I hadn't found them.*'

And I had a flash of Nanai – throwing her ship photo. Then I had another flash of the wall at Café Hoa – all those people, reunited with the people who'd saved them.

Suddenly, I understood something.

Last year, when Veronique's dad took her to the café, Nanai must have seen the photo of the ship, the same as the one on her bedside table. But had she ALSO noticed someone in one of the pictures? Someone who'd been brought to England?

And was she trying to find them?

I swallowed, and shook my head, really wanting to think about it – but I had to get ready for the next event.

It was the long jump. Daisy and I did it – and Billy, though he was hardly even trying. His go was pathetic, which was *so* frustrating. It was like he didn't care, just shaking his head and walking off when Mrs Martin went over to see if he was okay. He then refused to do the javelin, which was next, though he had to do the last race: the 800 metres. There were no heats, we just all went in one, Maeve Brennan coming second in the Year 3 race and another St Saviour's kid coming third! That meant we Year 4s HAD to do well. We couldn't rely on Daisy, though.

'TWICE round?' she said, gawping at the track. 'I've never even *thought* of running that far. I didn't even know that far *existed*.'

Veronique looked equally nervous, so I knew where our only chance lay: with Billy and me.

282

And to begin with it was okay. We all shuffled together at the start, elbowing each other, waiting for the pistol. When it went, we set off, the kid in spikes taking an early lead. Billy and I kept fairly close to him, though, in a jagged pack of seven or eight other kids. I felt good, knowing I could go faster if I wanted, pretty sure that even if we just kept this pace up we'd come in the top three or four. But when we were coming down the bottom bend, past the start, Billy just stopped! He came to a halt right in front of me! I crashed into the back of him, then grabbed his arm and started pulling him to get going again. He snatched it away, though, and shook his head.

'Come on!' I screamed. 'Billy, COME ON!'

'I can't,' he said, as the kids in our group ran past us. 'My stomach hurts. I . . .'

'You are so SELFISH!' I bellowed, as more kids swept past. And I knew I had a choice: either stand there and argue, or get on with it. So I shoved Billy out the way and sped up, SO ANGRY that I caught up with the last lot of kids who'd overtaken me, and then the little group I'd been in before.

And then it was strange. It was like I was being swept along, as if the track was moving beneath my feet like one of those flat escalators at the airport. I could see Spike Boy ahead. It was like he was all I *could* see, as if we were somehow attached by a piece of string. And I was reeling him in. Slowly he got closer, as if it wasn't me going *forward* but him coming *backwards*. I wouldn't catch him, not before the line. Would I? Were my feet actually touching the track? It was like I was floating, and then, incredibly, I was floating *past him*, my chest breaking right through the tape.

'YES!' Mrs Martin shouted. 'WELL DONE, CYMBELINE!'

And it was amazing. Everyone but Billy crowded round me, even the Year 3s – because we'd actually WON. Out of all the schools, we'd come FIRST, something that didn't seem real until we were standing on this podium with the biggest, shiniest cup I have EVER seen. The best thing was that Mrs Martin was Mrs Martin again, grinning from ear to ear. And Veronique was grinning too, helping to hoist up the cup as Mrs Martin took a photo.

Only one person wasn't into it.

Billy.

He'd been standing off to the side. Not that we cared – he could go and stuff himself. But as we were preparing to go, he turned to Mrs Martin.

'I think I'm going to be sick,' he said.

I rolled my eyes at that. It was *sooooo* pathetic. He was just making excuses. We'd all tried our hardest. Even Veronique had, and her granny was ill in hospital. I shook my head, hoping that Mrs Martin would just tell him to pull himself together – but again she took Billy seriously. Her face creased up and she held her hand to his forehead. When she said she'd go with him over to the loos I wanted to scream, 'No! Don't be nice to him! You don't know what I know! It was him!' But I just nodded when Mrs Martin turned away with Billy, telling us to wait in the car park.

'Come on,' Daisy said to the Year 3s. 'Losers.'

We'd got one point more than them.

So Billy didn't matter, did he? As long as he didn't go telling people at school that he'd won it for us of course.

We walked off to the car park, stopping only to look in the windows at the skateboard track, some big kids riding on it. I wanted to come back with my board.

'Didn't know you had one,' Daisy said.

I nodded. 'My dad got me it for Christmas.'

'Didn't know you had a dad either.'

'He's sort of part-time.'

'Right. Why've I never seen you on your board, then?'

'Mum. She won't let me use it outside.'

'*What?* Why not?'

'Boxing Day. We were at the top of Greenwich Park. I was trying to do an ollie but the skateboard ran away from me.'

'So?'

'It went down the hill.'

'Blimey. Did it hit anything?'

'Uh-huh.'

'What?'

'A puppy,' I said.

'No way!'

'Way. And the owner fell over trying to catch the board.'

'And did they?'

'No. It went on.'

'And?'

'It hit a cyclist.'

'*What?*'

'And a pigeon. And a remote-control car, three toddlers and Mrs Johnson.'

'Our last head teacher?'

'Then a vicar, before it rammed into a police car.'

'Cym! Did you get in trouble?'

'Mum made me go and collect it while she hid behind some bushes. The cyclist went mad. The mums were too busy holding their toddlers to be cross, though.'

'What about the vicar?'

'He was too busy holding his ankle.'

'Was he hurt?'

'The ambulance man said he thought it was broken.'

'The amb—? They took him to HOSPITAL?'

'Blue flashy lights and everything. He was okay, though. I reassured him.'

'How?'

'They were going to Lewisham so I patted him on the shoulder. "Tell them Cymbeline sent you," I said.'

We walked on, leaving the Year 3s to gawp in at the climbing wall. Round the back we stared: the car park was so big that we couldn't remember where Mrs Martin's car was. Daisy said past the main door so we walked on – which is when it happened. I can still see it. Daisy kicked something. She didn't mean to, it was just lying on the floor: a thin metal can. It spun forward and ricocheted off some car wheels before ending up at my feet. I picked it up, wondering what it was, Daisy trying to grab it to see too.

And that's when Mrs Martin came up with Billy.

Billy looked bad. But in a different way now. His eyes were wide open and Mrs Martin's were too. They were staring at something behind us, which made us

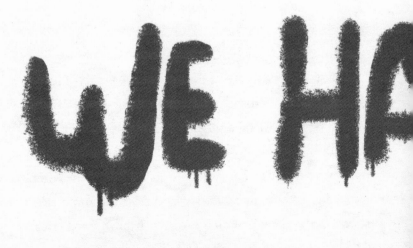

turn – just in time to see Mr Baker sweeping in to park. But they weren't staring at his car. They were staring at Mrs Martin's – which was different. It wasn't just white like it normally was.

It had writing on.

Red writing, scrawled all along the doors, and the windows, and the side of the bonnet. Big red spidery writing that said:

CHAPTER THIRTY-NINE

And Mr Baker was staring at it too.

He'd jumped out of his car and was standing there, stunned, until he stopped staring at Mrs Martin's car – and stared at us. Daisy and me, our hands clutched round the can I'd picked up from the floor which, I could see now, was a spray can.

With bright red drips running all the way down the side.

'*Daisy?*' Mrs Martin whispered. '*Cymbeline?*'

We couldn't move. Our hands were glued to the can until Daisy jumped back. But Mr Baker boomed at her.

'It's too late now, young lady! This is the MOST disgraceful thing I have *ever* seen. You two, get in my car. NOW!'

'But it wasn't them,' said Veronique.

'Come now,' hissed Mr Baker. 'Don't be ridiculous. LOOK at them.'

'But it wasn't,' insisted Veronique and I nodded, turning to Billy, who was almost completely white. 'I KNOW it wasn't.'

'How?' bellowed Mr Baker, as Veronique stepped forward, about, I was sure, to point at Billy, and FINALLY REVEAL THE TRUTH. But she didn't. Instead she lifted her chin and looked right into Mr Baker's big, red, shaking face.

'Because it was me,' she said.

CHAPTER FORTY

No one spoke on the way back. Mr Baker drove right down to the school gates (not allowed) and we got out, Veronique going straight into the office when he pointed that way.

'Classrooms,' he said to the rest of us, Billy running off ahead, seeming to be OKAY NOW. I went after him, but Daisy caught my arm.

'Wow!' she said. 'Can you believe that?'

'He's certainly fit enough *now*, isn't he?'

'No! Veronique! I accused her last week, but I didn't really mean it.'

'*What?*'

'But to think! Have you any idea why she's been doing it?'

I stared at Daisy, barely able to believe what she was saying. And I told her about Billy's party.

'Jelly? So what? Veronique ADMITTED it.'

Daisy pushed past me and went up to our classroom, barging the sticky door open while I stared after her in disbelief. It wasn't Veronique. NO WAY. Why she'd confessed, I had no idea, but IT WASN'T HER!

'Cymbeline!' said Mrs Stebbings, who had her coat on. 'How'd you get on?'

'We won.'

'That's terrific!'

'No, it's terrible,' I said.

And I thought of Veronique, back in Mr Baker's office.

And I thought about her for the rest of the day. I had to, because she didn't come out. When Mum picked me up Veronique was still in there, neither her mum nor her dad having come yet. I sent Mum in to ask if she could come home with us, but she came out and shook her head.

'We can't take her unless it's been agreed,' she explained. 'Why's she in with Mr Baker anyway? He seems cross. Has she done something?'

'NO,' I said.

Daisy came over then. 'Sorry, Cym. Mum says I've got to go to ballet tonight. Doesn't matter now anyway, does it?'

I opened my mouth to tell Daisy that it mattered even more. Not only did I have to speak to her dad again, we also HAD to talk about Mrs Martin. But Daisy had already disappeared.

'We can't just leave her,' I insisted, turning back to look at the office.

'Sorry,' Mum said, 'there really isn't anything we can do. Mr Baker said her mum's on her way. You can see Veronique tomorrow.'

But I couldn't.

When I got to school on Tuesday morning, Veronique wasn't there. And she didn't come in ALL DAY, though her name was certainly mentioned – in the corridors, the playground, the dining hall and the toilets.

'*What? Veronique?*'

'*In Year 4?*'

'*It was her?*'

'*That clever one?*'

'*No way!*'

'*Think she'll be expelled?*'

'*I hope so! Won't have to listen to any more of that piano, will we?*'

'*Cool to make that bag explode, though!*'

'*But why? Why WOULD she?*'

That last one came from Miss Phillips, whispering to Mr Ashe as they walked round to the ICT suite. I just stared after them and then looked round for someone else – *Billy*. But guess what? That little coward didn't come into school on Tuesday either.

Or Wednesday. And Veronique was still off too. It rained ALL day, the drip buckets plinking, Mrs Stebbings getting out some of her washing-up bowls as well because the problem was getting even worse, with water coming down into the library now, Mr Ashe having to move some of the books. The only good thing about that day was something I usually dread.

'Well *done*, Cymbeline,' Miss Phillips said as she handed our homework books back. 'ALL correct! You really are getting the hang of apostrophes.'

Lance laughed. 'Enjoy your sleepover at Veronique's?'

'She did NOT help me!' I said. 'She did NOT!'

That night, just as I had the day before, I *begged* Mum to call Veronique. But again she said no: we had to leave the family alone.

'But *why*?'

'It's . . . a special time for them. A serious time.'

'But Veronique won't *want* me to leave her alone.'

'I . . . I'm sorry, Cym. I've texted. I've sent our love. I've said that you want to speak to her. But we have to leave it up to them right now. Okay?'

It was NOT okay. I don't think Mum wanted me to talk to Veronique. By then, she'd found out what Veronique had confessed to and even *she* believed it.

'She's under a lot of stress,' she said. 'All the things she does. Piano, violin, fencing, Chinese, French. She's highly strung.'

'What does that mean?'

'She takes things very seriously. You know that. And with the added worry about her grandma, perhaps it was all too much.'

I just stared at Mum. Yes, I knew about Veronique, *and* I knew what people said about her. They didn't just call her Siri. The Year 5s called her Spock. The Year 6 boys called her Google Brain, while the girls just called her Weirdo. But she was great – and there was NO WAY she'd done those things.

'So,' I said, 'you actually believe it was her?'

'But she *said* so!'

I just glared at her before running up the stairs and slamming my bedroom door. When Mum knocked, I didn't answer. When she knocked again I shouted at her to leave me alone, which is when I saw the PSG shirt. It was lying on my bed. I yanked the door open.

'I tried it on. It doesn't fit.'

I shoved the shirt into Mum's chest and slammed the door again.

CHAPTER FORTY-ONE

Thursday: still no Veronique.

And still no Billy.

I was desperate. I kept pestering Mum so she did send a few more texts to Veronique's mum. The reply said Nanai was worse. She'd lost weight, she had an infection. When she was awake she wouldn't eat or talk, though mostly she just slept.

When Mum told me that, I ran up to my room again. She came after me and sat next to me on the bed. She told me that it was hard, hard for everyone, but that what was happening was also normal. And natural.

'No!' I said. 'You DON'T understand. There's something going on!' I was frantic. Time was running out. I could feel it. And it made me feel so powerless.

But there WERE things I could do.

That night, just like I had at Veronique's, I waited until Mum was asleep. When the house was silent, I got dressed and slid down the bannisters (our stairs creak too). Then I turned the key in the lock. I WASN'T going to let Veronique down. I'd go round there. Throw stones at her window. Together we could work it all out. I pulled the door open and a rush of cold air bit into my face. But an even colder voice snapped out behind me.

'WHAT ON EARTH DO YOU THINK YOU'RE DOING?'

Mum was SO angry. She pulled me into the living room, shaking so much that she could hardly talk. Until she said, 'You were going to walk round there? At night? On YOUR OWN?! Are you crazy?'

I said no. I just cared about Veronique and Nanai, when no one else seemed to AT ALL. But Mum said there was no excuse.

'You just can't do things like that,' she said, clenching her fists with worry, and relief. Then she locked the front door, took the key out, and shoved it into the pocket of her dressing gown.

*

The next day was Friday. I got to school early, but there was still no Veronique. And no Billy. It made me wonder if he was actually ill. I hoped so, and with something PAINFUL, though I still had to speak to him. I had to make him confess so that Veronique could come back: then we could talk about Nanai. Because, what if people were right? What if Veronique HAD been expelled? Or what if Mr Baker was thinking of expelling her? Being in the dark was SO frustrating, and as soon as I got into class I went up to Miss Phillips's desk.

'I'm sorry,' she said, 'I can't say anything. All I know is that the governors are meeting on Saturday to discuss some other things. Maybe they'll talk about it then.'

'But that's TOMORROW!'

'Yes, but—'

'It's not fair!' I said.

'Well, I'm sorry,' she said. 'Now go and sit down, please.'

And I was going to – but I had an idea.

'No!'

'I beg your pardon?'

'NO! I WON'T. You all just think it's her, and it's not! You don't care about her! No one does!'

'Cymbeline, take your *seat,* please.'

'I won't! And you can't make me! It's a disgrace! All of you, you're horrible. You're just all horrible, I tell you!'

'Cymbeline,' warned Miss Phillips, but I didn't stop. As everyone in the class stared at me, I screamed and I screamed and I SCREAMED.

And five minutes later I was at the door of Mr Baker's office.

School still hadn't started yet. Mr Baker was talking on his phone. He waved Miss Phillips in without looking up and she sat me in the chair opposite his desk. He put his hand over his phone as, very quickly, she told him what I'd done. He nodded and waved her out, carrying on talking as she left, going through papers on his desk at the same time. Was he discussing Veronique? With one of the governors? Were they planning what to do with her? He became so engrossed that he forgot about me, looking startled when he glanced up five minutes later and saw me there.

'Can you hold on?' he said (to his phone). 'Actually, I'll call you back.' He scribbled a number down, hung up, and looked at me.

'Right,' he said. 'Coriolanus?'

'Cymbeline.'

'Of course. Well, you, er, you really shouldn't.'

'I shouldn't . . . ?'

'No. You need to listen to, er, Miss Phillips. And pay attention, and that sort of thing. And definitely not . . .'

'Yes, Mr Baker?'

'Do . . .'

'Yes?'

'What it was that she just told me you did. Not good, okay?'

'Okay.'

'And . . .'

But Mr Baker's phone went again before he could go on. He shook his head, answered it, and then put his free hand over his spare ear. Motioning me to wait there, he stood up, came round his desk and went out, listening and nodding all the time.

YES!

I stood. My heart pounding, I glanced through the window. Mr Baker was walking out towards the road, still talking, the odd late kid hurrying in around him. As fast as I could I turned to his desk. Sending my eyes this way and that, I scanned the papers, looking for something, *anything*, about Veronique. But there were just drawings of the school, some normal, others that looked like school but didn't at the same time. I remembered the letter I'd taken home, and sighed. Drat! It was probably about that, or else Mr Baker was planning renovations to stop all the drips. The only thing that *might* have been relevant was the number Mr Baker had scribbled down. It was on a memo pad, and I picked up Mr Baker's desk phone and squinted at the note – his handwriting was worse than Lance's. When I'd managed to decipher it, I dialled and held the receiver to my ear.

'Hello?' a woman's voice said. 'Roger?'

Roger? Above Mr Baker's desk there was a teaching certificate hanging on the wall. *Roger Baker.*

'Roger?' the voice said again. 'Can you hear me? Mike's on the other line. Do you want to wait? Actually, I *thought* he was talking to you! Hello? *Roger?*'

I hung up, then ran back round and sat down again – just as Mr Baker came back.

'Right,' he said, 'off you go. And no more of it, okay?'

I said okay, but I wanted to scream again – because I knew who the woman on the other end of the line was.

Billy's mum.

Was she a governor? Or was his dad? Veronique was sunk! Instead of screaming, though, I just turned and went off to assembly, on the off chance that Veronique would be there.

But she wasn't.

Though Billy *was*, sitting cross legged next to Marcus Breen.

When I glared at Billy, he stared back like a frightened rabbit. All day he avoided me, staying in at first play, then again at lunchtime, with Mr Ashe in the library. At last play I got him, though. I went to the library and in a loud voice asked Mr Ashe if I could help sort books. Billy heard me and went outside. Then, when Mr Ashe wasn't looking, I snuck out after him.

The playground was full, people going on as normal, as if nothing was happening. I shook my head at that and then jogged over to the top end, where the usual kids were playing football. Marcus and Darren Cross were there, lots of Year 5s and 3s. But – weirdly – Billy wasn't. He was nowhere in fact – until I thought to look behind the shed.

And he was sitting there, staring at his phone (in Year 4, I know).

'Cym . . .' He swallowed and jerked up. 'You have to believe me.'

'Believe you, *what*?'

'Please,' he said, 'you have to.'

'WHAT?'

'It wasn't me.'

Billy was sitting on an old chair and I towered over him, my fingers curling into fists, so strange because – if he'd wanted to – Billy could pound my head in.

But he was *cowering*.

'You're a liar.'

'I'm not!' he said, before doing something that threw me. He started crying. Billy did! He cried and cried, his phone pressed against his forehead until – TOTALLY FREAKED OUT AT THIS POINT – I walked backwards and turned into the playground. Where Daisy was chatting to Vi. Almost in a daze, I stumbled over and pulled her to the side.

'A playdate?' she said, when I told her what I wanted. 'Tonight?'

I nodded. 'We *have* to.'

'But why?'

I nearly said *because of Nanai! Because of Veronique!* But I caught myself in time. 'The Lewisham

Cup. It starts *tomorrow*. We *need* to train. If we do well, we'll be in the starting seven all season.'

Daisy's eyes lit up but she sighed. 'Friday's family night. We have to eat supper together. It is SO boring. Come round in the morning, early. Matches don't start till 10.30, do they?'

It was the best I was going to get, so I walked away, wishing I hadn't had to lie to Daisy. It couldn't be helped, though – I absolutely HAD to find out what her dad had been doing visiting Nanai.

And I was going to do it the very next day.

CHAPTER FORTY-TWO

In the morning, Mum stopped the car outside Daisy's house. She said she was going shopping but she'd be there for the matches.

'And Stephan's coming too!'

I shrugged, Mum waiting until Daisy had answered the door before she drove away.

'Is your dad in?' I said.

Daisy opened the door wider and I went in, remembering their house from the one time I'd been there. That was a party, though, and I hadn't remembered how unbelievably tidy it was. After I'd taken my shoes off, Daisy picked them up and put them on a rack which had her name on, as well as her brothers' names, in rows. The coat pegs had names above them too. Daisy told me to hang mine on the one that said 'Visitors', but I couldn't reach so she did it for me, and then we walked through a hall that was COMPLETELY clear (no bikes, books, homework folders, slippers or schoolbags *anywhere*). Their kitchen (down some stairs) was the same: the worktops clean, jars neatly lined up for tea, coffee, sugar, flour, rice, and so on. The chairs were all neat, and there were no party invites or Tesco vouchers on the fridge door, which was open. In fact, there was only one thing on it: a family planner. I stared at this. It too was split up into people. On today's date, under Daisy's column, it said:

!!! **FOOTBALL** !!!
10.30 - Markham Park
11.30 - Ashtead Grove

Under her brother Johnny's name it said 'Swimming', and Milo had a party later. Astrid (her mum) had something called 'Pilates' that day, while under Graham (her dad) it said:

Afternoon –
Watching the golf
LEAVE ME ALONE

So did he write down *everything*? I was wondering this when the fridge door shut and he was standing there.

'Bit early, isn't it, Cymbeline?' he said. 'What can we do for you?'

Daisy walked past me. 'He's here to play foot—'

'Can you tell me more about your job, please?' I said.

'My!' Mr Blake poured milk into a mug of coffee and sat down at the table. 'You *are* keen. My own kids, not so much. I could be an exotic dancer for all they'd care. Long as I kept them in phones and laptops, of course. Which bits of my fascinating profession are you interested in today?'

'Finding people,' I said – because I'd worked it out. Or thought I had. Last night I'd gone through everything I knew and it all came down to this: Veronique's dad had said that Nanai had been to Café Hoa. She'd looked at the pictures and it was all too much for her – especially the ones of *people who'd been rescued – and the people who'd rescued them.*

Some time later, a photo of Veronique had gone missing from the living room and ended up in Nanai's footstool, and Daisy's dad had come to see her, after which Nanai had (1) stopped eating and (2) thrown a photo of the ship that had rescued her, breaking the frame.

All of which led to one question: what, or who, had she seen in those photos in the café?

Was it to do with the ship? Or someone else who had been *on* the ship? Maybe it was even one of the British Navy officers who had rescued her – had she seen him in the photo and then gone looking for him? I didn't know, but it felt like the top cupboard in our kitchen where Mum keeps all the chocolate – it was there but out of my reach.

'Ah, the old-fashioned stuff.'

'That's right. How do you do it?'

'Satnav. Just type in the road.'

'Sorry?'

'A joke, though – blimey – do they make life easier now. No, you just need to be organised. And there are various records you can use. Birth registers, marriage registers . . .'

'What have you used recently?'

'Let me see . . . A young chap had an inheritance coming and I used driving licence records.'

'Anything else?'

'The electoral roll. It shows where people live. Only useful if you know where to look, though.'

'What about military records?'

'What do you mean?'

'Like, maybe, perhaps . . .'

'Spit it out.'

'*Navy* records?'

'That's funny,' he said, 'I *have* actually looked at some of those recently.'

YES! 'When?'

'And written *tons* of letters.'

'What kind?'

'Well, if you're looking for someone from a particular group of people, you write letters to places where that person might be.'

Letters? Navy records? I was close, I knew it. 'So if you think you know where someone is, you go there?'

'Sometimes.'

'That must be really interesting – going to new places.'

'Can be. Went to France last year.'

'Wow. But what about . . . ?'

'Yes?'

'More recently?' I said, my eyes flicking over to the family planner. And Daisy's dad was about to answer. He really was. His eyes went up as he thought about it, his mouth opening to speak – but Daisy ruined it.

'I THOUGHT we were going to play football,' she said.

That put her dad off and he asked what she meant. She told him about the Cup starting and how we wanted to practise. 'Great!' he said. 'I'll come too,' and he hurried up the stairs to get changed.

I hissed out a sigh, raging with frustration. I wanted to go over to the planner – but Daisy dragged me up the stairs. She got a ball and some cones from under her stairs and pulled open the front door. 'Dad can catch us up,' she said. I was surprised she was allowed out on her own but we weren't going far. There's a little park right by their house, and it was empty but for some dogs running about and two people with raincoats on, and plastic bags instead of gloves. Daisy set the cones out for dribbling and I went first.

'Are you all right?' she said.

'Sorry.' I sighed, and put three of the cones back up.

'You seem distracted.'

'It's nothing.'

Daisy put her hands on her hips. 'Cym?'

'Yes?'

She squinted at me. 'Do you *really* want to be a policeman?'

I shrugged. 'Maybe.'

'Well, I'm going to be a footballer,' she said. 'You boys all *say* you're going to be, going on about your heroes. But I actually *am*.'

I went in goal while Daisy dribbled round the cones and smacked it past me. Then her dad came, and though I tried to get the subject back to where he'd been recently, I couldn't. He kept going on about tactics, teaching us how to spin off the defenders or use a drag back to get free from the wing. He told us that if it started raining like it was threatening then we should get loads of shots in. Again I tried to get him back to his job, but he wasn't interested. I told myself it didn't matter: if I could maybe just get back into their kitchen . . . but Daisy's dad said it was time to head off.

'Really?'

'Yep. They'll want you there early to warm up.'

'And we don't want to be late,' Daisy said. She picked up the cones and stacked them.

'But . . . don't we need to take water?'

'Got it,' her dad said.

'Our bags?'

'Popped them in the car just now.'

'Come on!' Daisy said, the ball under her arm now. She turned and marched off, her dad following, while I sighed. Their car was right outside their house and Daisy's dad unlocked it. Daisy pulled the back door open and climbed in, beckoning me to follow. But I stopped.

'What's the *matter*?'

'Who are we playing today?'

She grimaced. 'Doesn't matter. We'll smash them anyway.'

'Be good to know, though,' her dad said.

Daisy sighed. 'Why?'

'Just would,' I said. 'Shows we're prepared.'

'If you say so. I did write it down.'

'Where?'

'On our planner. It's on our fridge. But . . .'

'I'll go!' I shouted, backing out of the car and running over to the door before Daisy could grab me.

Daisy's mum was coming out with her brother Johnny, so she let me in – and I scampered down the stairs. For a second I stopped, because Daisy's other brother was at the table – but he was looking at his phone and eating Frosties. He didn't even notice me. I edged round him and up to the fridge: Markham Park, Ashtead Grove. But I already knew that, so I turned the pages back.

One week.

Then another.

And four words burned themselves into my brain.

Sea View Care Home

CHAPTER FORTY-THREE

So THIS was the answer.

THIS was the place Daisy's dad had gone, *the day before going to see Nanai*. I stared, hardly able to believe it – though where WAS the Sea View Care Home? And *who* was there?

'Cymbeline!' called Daisy's dad. 'What are you doing down there? Baking a cake?!'

I let the page fall against the wall and ran back up the stairs.

'Mr Blake,' I said, 'about your work. Whereabouts exactly . . . ?'

'Come on!' urged Daisy, from the car.

And it seemed that even her dad didn't mess with Daisy, because he turned round and hurried into the driver's seat, without answering me.

It's only a five-minute drive to the heath from there and Mr Blake spent it giving us more advice. And when we arrived, he stayed where he was.

'Going to get coffee,' he said. 'I'll be there for kick-off, though.'

I sighed, climbed out, and watched him drive away. And then I looked out on the scene in front of us, the big patch of grass I'd played football on *so many* times. But it was different today. There were parents. Cars. There were all the kids from the other schools in their different kits. Then there were the pitches, with PROPER lines instead of cones and REAL goals with REAL nets instead of schoolbags or poles. Daisy's eyes lit up like stars and mine should have done too: I'd been dreaming of this day for YEARS. But it hardly seemed real.

Sea View Care Home?

WHERE WAS IT?

I had to find out. And soon. That morning, Mum had been on the phone to Veronique's mum. They'd been whispering, and it can't have been good news. If it was, she'd have told me. So what could I do? Vi's dad was getting some balls out, so I ran over – and told him

I'd forgotten my shin pads. He sighed and handed over his phone for me to call Mum. I didn't call her, though. Instead I went on to the Internet, not really expecting it to work. But it did, and almost immediately. And I Googled 'Sea View Care Home'.

YES!

'Sea View Care Home, Falmouth,' I read. There was an address, a website and everything!

But where was Falmouth? Was it close? Could I get there now? I tapped Vi's dad on the arm, about to hand him the phone back and ask him, but I stopped. Because under the listing for that Sea View Care Home was *another* Sea View Care Home. It was in Cardiff. And that was Wales! So which one had Mr Blake gone to? I was about to wonder that – until I saw more. There was a Sea View Care Home in Southend, wherever that was. There was also one in Shoreham, and one in Whitstable, one in Deal, Aberdeen, Bournemouth and Aberystwyth. And there were more. So which was the right one? How could I POSSIBLY know? Mr Blake wouldn't tell me. Did I just have to phone them all up? I didn't know.

But someone might.

'Thanks,' I said, handing the phone back to Vi's

dad. And when he turned his back, I legged it.

I had somewhere to be, and it wasn't at football.

I sprinted across the grass. Where the road narrows I stopped, until a woman in a Mini let me cross (THANKS!) and I sprinted down the hill. At the pelican crossing outside Blackheath station I waited for the Charlton player to turn green and then ran up the hill on the other side. Then I turned left, and stopped again.

Outside Blackheath Music Centre.

A boy was going in. His dad was behind him, carrying a guitar. I followed, catching the heavy door before it shut, then staying behind the dad when they walked up to the reception.

And I listened.

From a room on my left came the squeak of a violin. There were drums coming from a room on my right, and a ukulele somewhere. Then – YES! It was faint, but definitely there. A piano.

A piano that was being played BRILLIANTLY.

I turned. The sound was coming from above me. The receptionist was still talking to the man so I leapt up the stairs, more violins sounding on the first floor, and a flute: but no piano. I went up again, and then again, until I emerged into a small foyer. And I could hear it. Loud. From a door ahead of me, which I stared at until, glancing to my left, I saw another door which was open and revealed parents. They were chatting, obviously waiting for their kids – and Veronique's mum was one of them.

She wasn't chatting, though. Mrs Chang was just sitting there, staring into space, her face all serious and heavy. So was I too late? Was all this effort for nothing? Something inside my stomach seemed to slump but I fought it. And before Mrs Chang could see me I rushed forward to the other door, grabbed the handle and shoved.

'Cymbeline?' said Veronique, turning round on her piano stool.

Veronique's eyes were WIDE. Kit-Kat was on her shoulder and he looked surprised too, though not half as surprised as the woman who was sitting at a table behind them. She was tall. Her grey hair was piled on her head like a chimney. And she wasn't happy at ALL.

She asked me what on !EARTH! I was doing. She told me that this was an !EXAMINATION! She said I had to leave !IMMEDIATELY! But I didn't. Instead I told Veronique everything – all the things, in fact, that

I should have been telling her all along. Kit-Kat held his paw up for a high-five and I gave it to him, just as I got to the bit about Daisy's family planner, and the trip Daisy's dad had taken the day before he visited Nanai.

'And that's where he went?' asked Veronique. 'To the Sea View Care Home?'

'YES! Have you heard of it?'

'No,' said Veronique.

DRAT!

'But what about the town?'

'The . . . ?'

'TOWN! There are LOADS of Sea View care homes – Southend, Falmouth, Aberystwyth, Aberdeen – loads of towns and cities all over the place. So I thought that one place might mean something to you. Maybe from something Nanai has said. That's why I came running. Well?'

But Veronique shrugged. 'No, I don't *think* so. Though . . .'

'WHAT?'

Veronique jumped up, her eyes wide. '*Sea* View?' she said.

'Yes.'

'Then I know just where to look!'

And Veronique leapt away from the piano, shoved me to the side, and RAN!

'!WAIT!' squawked the woman with the chimney. 'You've only played !TWO PIECES! You haven't even done your !SIGHT READING!'

CHAPTER FORTY-FOUR

But Veronique was already out of the door, and before I was out too she'd legged it down the stairs! At the bottom, the door was still swinging so I dodged through it, not catching sight of Veronique until she was crossing by the station, Kit-Kat clinging on to her jumper for dear life. Wondering where she was going, I chased her, up past the grocer's and over the narrow bit of road (another Mini – THANKS!). Ten metres behind, I watched as she sprinted across the grass – up to Lance? No. He was doing headers with Darren Cross and she went past him. Billy? No. He and Marcus were drinking from water bottles and she ignored them too.

And found Daisy.

But what was the point? Her dad wouldn't tell us!

Veronique seemed to have a plan, though, because she was shouting at Daisy – and when I got close I could hear her.

'When did you get it?' Veronique shrieked.

'Get it?'

'Yes,' insisted Veronique, though Daisy didn't answer. Instead she frowned, and not just because she didn't know what ON EARTH Veronique was on about. She still thought Veronique was the one who'd attacked Mrs Martin!

'Well? Tell me! *Please.*'

And she pointed at the stick of rock which, once again, was rooted in Daisy's hand.

'Please!' I panted, when I got there.

'All right. If *you*'re asking.'

'So?'

'I got it two weeks ago. But so what?'

'On *Saturday*?'

'Yeah. My dad got them. He . . .'

But Daisy didn't get to finish – because Veronique tore the stick of rock right out of her hand!

Daisy fought her, but Veronique managed to hold her off (probably due to all that fencing). I just watched in amazement as she stared at the stick of rock – at the sucked end, which was all pointy now, and shiny. After that she sighed, and then she did something unbelievable. Taking the rock in both hands she brought her knee up – and snapped it!

'**AAAARRRRRGGGGGHHHHHHHHH!!!!!!!!!!**'

Daisy bellowed!

And I could understand! Was everyone right about Veronique? *Was* she crazy? She shoved one of the ends towards me.

'No thanks!' I said. 'Not after Daisy's licked it! And you really shouldn't have . . .'

'No!' screamed Veronique, twisting away again from Daisy.

And I saw it.

The word.

It ran right through the rock!

All the way from one end to the other.

Not Falmouth or Cardiff or Aberdeen.

CHAPTER FORTY-FIVE

'Is it close?' I said. Veronique didn't answer for a second. She had to give the rock-ends back to Daisy, and when she did, she winced.

'No.'

'No?'

She shook her head. 'It's on the south coast. Population two hundred and twenty thousand. Britain's first Green Party MP. Famous for the Royal Pavilion.'

'But is it NEAR here?'

'*No!* It's miles away.'

'Then what are we going to do?!'

'Pardon?'

'What can we *do*? We have to get there, to find out what stopped Nanai eating.'

'*What?*'

'I said, how can we *get* there? Who'll take us? Nanai's REALLY ill. Your mum called my mum. They might not have told you, because of your exam.'

'WHAT?'

'On the phone! I heard Mum sighing. We have to *get* there!'

'*WHAT?!!!*'

'I said, we . . .'

'It's no good! I CAN'T HEAR YOU! I CAN'T HEAR YOU!' screamed Veronique.

And then, weirdly, I couldn't hear Veronique either.

Because of the rumbling sound.

Was it thunder? Was the weather worse than Daisy's dad thought? It got louder, an insistent thudding. Was it an earthquake? Yes! It must be – because balls were rolling past me on their own! Cones were tripping along, orange bibs streaming over the grass while kids and parents ran past. I stared, in amazement, as the whole Markham Park team crashed into Ashtead Grove, and Lance tripped over the kit bag. Marcus Breen ran into a goalpost as the thudding got worse, and WORSE, the whole world seeming to shake as I stared, bewildered, jagging my eyes around, panic about to take me until Veronique grabbed hold of my wrist.

And pointed up.

At the helicopter.

The red helicopter.

And here's something else you won't believe. The helicopter moved back a bit, then landed, its rotor blades slowing with a *whump*.

And then a man got out.

In a red tracksuit.

And after saying hello he put his hands on his hips and studied us all.

'Right,' he said (with a grin), 'which one of you guys is Cymbeline?'

CHAPTER FORTY-SIX

I stared. I mean I REALLY stared. At Jacky Chapman. My hero.

And, right now, the hero I really *needed*.

Then I put my hand up.

Jacky Chapman beamed. 'Fantastic! Got your letter. Happy to give you a ride. No match today but shall we go and see the training ground?'

'Can some other people come?'

'Like your dad? Sure!'

'Sort of,' I said.

Veronique got on first. Then Mum, who'd just arrived and was staring at me like, *what on EARTH*? But it was hard to catch up with the noise of the helicopter. Stephan was next. His littlest girl was crying, though, so he got back out and stayed on the ground. Then I got on (in the seat next to the pilot's) and I thought Vi's dad was going to climb on too because he came running up to the door.

'But, Cymbeline!' he said.

'What?'

'You're in the starting seven!'

I was pleased. I was SO pleased. But it just couldn't be helped. I said sorry, suggested Lizzie Fisher instead, and Jacky Chapman went to shut the door – but Veronique's mum pulled it open!

'Veronique!' she said. 'What on earth—?'

'Just get in!' Veronique shouted, and Mum helped pull her on board.

We all put on headphones then – and two minutes later we were airborne. Two minutes *later* we were above our school, which made it very easy to see the state of our roof. There were big holes! Tiles were missing all over the place! No wonder we needed those drip buckets! Then we went higher, until the school was a Lego house, the whole of Blackheath a Subbuteo pitch.

'So,' said Jacky Chapman (the best captain Charlton have ever had). 'What do you think?'

I squinted at him. 'You're not as tall as I thought you'd be.'

'Oh.'

'And it took you AGES to get back to me.'

'Sorry. I did get your letter, but . . .'

'And the forwards should press more. Like Liverpool.'

'Right. I'll tell them. You can do it yourself if you like. At the training ground.'

'No!' I shouted.

And I told Jacky Chapman about Nanai (leaving out the fact that I'd replaced him with her on my Person Project). I told him how amazing she was. I told him what I'd just told Veronique, adding that Nanai had been a refugee and that she'd stopped eating, adding the stuff about the wall at Café Hoa where she must have seen something that had upset her, someone she'd known or someone who'd helped to rescue her maybe, and about the photo of the ship, and then about how Daisy's dad had gone to see her, and Daisy's stick of rock.

Veronique's mum gasped because she was hearing it all for the first time too.

Jacky Chapman whistled.

'And you're trying to save her?'

'YES!'

'Well, let's go then!'

And so we flew to Brighton. We flew over houses and fields, roads and hills: the country I lived in with all the different people in it. All just trying to get along. And after a while I realised that up ahead I could see the sea, which some people had to cross in various parts of the world just to be safe like we were, bringing with them their skills and talents, their music and food. And I wondered who would choose to live by the sea – who we might find at the Sea View Care Home. Might it be one of the Navy sailors from the ship that had rescued Nanai? Someone who'd spent their whole life on the sea, doing something amazing: rescuing people, helping them to a new life. People like Nanai, who didn't have much of that life left.

I didn't know *what* we would find. But we had to try, for Nanai.

We flew over some big green hills. We flew over a fancy white building that Veronique said was called the Royal Pavilion. We flew along the shore where thin brown fingers reached out into the sea. Then we got lower, and lower, a park below us, Jacky Chapman chatting on his radio then looking at his satnav.

And we landed in the park.

'That's it!' called out Veronique, pointing towards a low, modern building just beyond the park gates.

And it was.

After leaving Kit-Kat with some peas, we clambered out. And Veronique was right. There was a sign outside the building:

'Come on!' I shouted.

Mum was feeling woozy so she lagged behind as Veronique and I raced ahead. We ran in through the open gates and up to a glass door. There was a buzzer on the side and a voice from a speaker asked who we wanted to visit. I shrugged until the voice asked us again.

'Er, Grandad?' I said.

And the door clicked open.

Mum and Veronique's mum and Jacky Chapman came then. And we all went in. They went up to the reception desk as Veronique and I hurried past, figuring that that would be fine. No one stopped us.

I'd never been in a care home before but it was nice, with wide corridors and pictures on the walls, a little library on the left where two old ladies were chatting. They smiled at us and we smiled back, and went on, staring at the doors on either side of us. Each one had a name on – but we didn't *know* what name we were looking for! We had no idea who we'd come to see.

So what could we do?

'We just have to go back to reception,' said Veronique. 'And explain. Find out who Daisy's dad visited.'

'Okay,' I said. And I was about to – but we'd walked round a corner and an open door faced us. Through it was a much bigger room – with people in. Old people. They were mostly in comfy chairs, chatting or sleeping, some playing cards, others looking at the telly. We stood for a second, casting our eyes around, Veronique hissing out a sigh.

'We're so close,' she said. 'But how do we know who we're looking for?'

'I don't *know*. Maybe . . .'

'What?'

I shrugged. 'He'll have a sailor's hat on?'

'*What?*'

'Well, *I* don't know, do I!? I was just thinking. Or maybe he'll have a beard. Sailors sometimes do . . .

'*Sailors?*' said Veronique. 'What do sailors have to do with anything?'

'I just thought . . . maybe the person Nanai was looking for was one of the sailors who rescued her. She saw *something* at Café Hoa that started all this.'

Veronique blinked. 'She saw *something*, yes. I think you're right. But we have no idea what it was. Or WHO it was.'

My stomach sank. She was right.

There was probably no point even being here at all.

But then Veronique turned her head – and her eyes went wide. She walked off while I stared after her.

'Where are you going?' I said.

But Veronique didn't answer. She just marched forward into the big room while I looked round again, studying the old people. There weren't any sailor's hats, *or* beards. So which one was the one that Nanai had seen on the wall of Café Hoa? How could I tell?

Some were hunched over in their chairs, others sitting up straighter. One man was sending a text on his phone, another was reading a book and laughing. So did I just go round each one? Did I just say, 'Hello, did you know my friend's granny from Vietnam?'

I guessed I had to, and I wanted Veronique's help – but she'd wandered off to the far side of the room where music was playing. Heavens! Yes, I knew she liked it, but this was important!

'*Veronique!*' I hissed.

Veronique ignored me, though. So I followed her, further annoyed when I saw where she was going. She was walking up to a big set of closed glass doors where a little radio (the source of the music) sat on a small table, next to a high-backed chair. The chair was empty though so there was no one to ask, and I was about to make that point when I realised that it wasn't the music that had drawn her. It was the table.

It had a photo on it. And the photo was of a ship.

Nanai's ship.

CHAPTER FORTY-SEVEN

Everything stopped.

I was struck – *dead* still – and so was Veronique.

We both stared down at the photo before Veronique lifted her head and looked around the room. Then she drew her gaze back to the empty chair, while I swallowed. So. This was it. Whoever had sat in this chair was the person Nanai had seen in the photo.

This was where Daisy's dad had come – *but only to find the chair empty*. And *that*'s why he'd returned to Nanai and given her back the photograph of Veronique.

Because he had been too late.

Which meant that *we* were too late too.

The thought hit me like a punch. I didn't move. I couldn't move. I just stood there, as the backs of my eyes began to prickle, Veronique not moving either. Her shoulders slumped, her hands fell to her sides. And then both our mums came, and Jacky Chapman too. Mum started to speak, but when she saw the empty chair she stopped. I heard her take a deep breath and then felt her hand on my shoulder. I heard Veronique's mum sigh, like air going out of a punctured ball.

And then we were all silent, until some light from outside made me glance through the French windows. The sun had come out. A golden wand of light was firing down on to the big, grey, rumbling sea. And I wondered: were there people out there right now, cold and scared, needing help? I pictured Nanai, rescued from her little boat, and I pictured her now in her hospital bed – and how I'd FAILED to rescue her. By being too late. And I wanted to leave. I wanted us all to go. I'd dragged Veronique and her mum all the way here for nothing, when they could have been spending this time with Nanai.

'Come on,' I said.

But Veronique grabbed my wrist. And she pulled me round.

To see someone walking towards us.

It wasn't an old man, though. It was an old lady – a

really old lady – using the backs of the chairs to guide her across the room.

I stood and watched her, until she looked up and stopped.

'Who are you?' she said. Staring at me.

'I'm Cymbeline.'

'Really?' The old lady frowned, the lines on her forehead like a closed fan. 'What sort of name is *that*?'

'Oh, it's Shakespeare.'

'I know that! I'm not completely gaga, you know. Could have been worse, I suppose. Imagine, you could have been called Hamlet.'

'I know. Or . . . Romeo.'

'Well, then.' She turned her head. 'And you are?'

'Jacky Chapman,' (said Jacky Chapman).

'And you?'

'I'm that one's mum. Cymbeline's.'

'Right.'

'And I'm *her* mum,' said Veronique's mum.

'I see. So that just leaves you, young lady,' she said, turning to Veronique. She paused. 'And you are . . . ?'

But the old lady didn't go on. She stopped. Still. And she stared at Veronique – through eyes I suddenly recognised.

Eyes I'd seen before.

Veronique's eyes, but which were not on Veronique, but on this old lady. This lady with straight white hair and blotches on her face like thumbprints, the rest of her skin crisscrossed with loads and loads of tiny, straight lines.

Like an impossible game of Pick-up Sticks.

CHAPTER FORTY-EIGHT

'I'm Veronique,' said Veronique.

To my AMAZEMENT, the old lady lifted her hands and held them to the sides of Veronique's face. And she studied Veronique, just studied her like a painting, until a tear stepped carefully out of her left eye, then picked its way down her face.

'Oh yes,' she said. 'I *know*. I know exactly who you are.'

'Then . . .' Veronique swallowed. 'Who are you?'

'Thu,' whispered the old lady. 'My name is Thu. And I am your grandmother's sister.'

SILENCE.

SILENCE THAT WAS

SO LOUD.

SILENCE FOR WHAT

FELT LIKE

HOURS.

'But . . .' Veronique blinked. 'Why haven't we met before?'

'I didn't know which country your grandmother was brought to. And *she* thought I had drowned.'

'Yes,' said Veronique. 'Yes, she did.'

'Until she saw the photo,' I said.

Thu turned to me. 'Sorry?'

'She saw you in a photo, at Café Hoa,' I said. 'Standing by the ship that rescued you. In England. So she sent Daisy's dad to find you.' As I said it, I realised it was true. I couldn't believe I'd thought the person she'd seen had been a sailor.

'Daisy's dad?'

'The private investigator?'

'Oh. Yes.'

'But . . .' I frowned. 'Why did she stop eating, after he found you and went back to see her?'

Thu stared. 'She stopped eating?'

'Yes. She's in hospital.'

The old woman looked horrified. 'Then we should go to her. And . . . and I will explain. Everything. But I have to speak to Nanai first.

'Come on, then!'

CHAPTER FORTY-NINE

And fifteen minutes later, Thu met the last member of our band.

'This is Kit-Kat,' Veronique said, fastening her seatbelt and holding him up.

'He's a hamster,' Mum explained. 'Though he really is quite big, isn't he?'

'Eats too many peas,' I said.

You're not allowed to land on the roof of Lewisham Hospital. Jacky Chapman made that clear as we took off again, rain swiping against the helicopter's windows.

'But we HAVE to!'

'Sorry, only the air ambulance can do that.'

'But we are an air ambulance!!'

Jacky Chapman nodded and got on the radio to the hospital. We all listened as he explained.

'Well, I'm sorry,' the voice crackled. 'I can't allow it. Private aircraft are simply not permitted.'

'But this is an emergency!' I screamed.

'Be that as it may, it's just not . . .'

'DO YOU KNOW WHO I AM?'

There was a short silence. 'Sorry? Do I know who you . . . ?'

'I'm CYMBELINE!'

'What?!'

'*Igloo*.'

'Well, why didn't you SAY?' the voice asked.

And half an hour later the rotor blades were *whumping* to a stop again.

I got out first, rain lashing me in the face. Jacky Chapman was next, and then the rest climbed out the back.

Until only the old lady was left.

Jacky Chapman helped her out and the man we'd spoken to guided us towards an open door (after he'd shaken my hand). We hurried into a lift, down two floors, and out on to the corridor I'd been in before. Then we turned into the ward. There were more old people – in chairs, beds and wheelchairs, the same woman I'd seen before, staring at the ceiling. But where was Nanai? I spun around and stared at the bed she'd been lying in when I'd last seen her, and it was like the floor had suddenly vanished beneath my feet.

The bed was empty.

I took a breath. I stared at the smooth clean sheets, so very flat, and empty, the whole world seeming to come to a complete stop.

Until a voice said, 'Cymbeline?'

It was Veronique's dad. And I didn't know what to say to him. But then I realised that he was standing up from beside a bed on the other side of the ward.

And in that bed was Nanai.

Nanai was propped up against some pillows. Asleep. And ill-looking. SO ill-looking, her face thin, her arms limp. She'd looked so old last time I'd seen her there but now she looked far, far beyond old. Mr Chang was next to her and he stared, his eyes wide as dinner plates when he saw us walking towards him.

'But . . .' he said.

'Yes?'

'But that's . . .'

'Yes?'

349

'Jacky Chapman!'

'I know. And . . .' I stepped out of the way. 'This is Thu. Nanai! This is Thu! It's your *sister*, Nanai.'

Veronique's dad asked how that could possibly be, but Veronique's mum held up her hand to him and guided the old lady – Thu – to a chair. And Thu sat, staring down at her sister, her hands immediately finding one of Nanai's. She gripped it while I stared, looking round as a nurse came up. She wanted to know what was happening and who we all were, telling us we were too many, saying we needed to be quiet because Nanai was *very* poorly.

But she stopped mid-sentence. Thu held up *her* hand, staring down at Nanai as I wondered, *Is this it?* Is this all she'll get to do, just look at the sister she hasn't seen for so long? Will she never get to speak to Nanai and laugh with her, never get to properly *be* with her again? Thu seemed to be having the same thought because she gasped, pain on her face that told me this was even worse for her then not seeing Nanai at all. But then her face changed. Her eyes opened like she was remembering something, something from long, long ago, digging it out of a past that she'd thought was lost to her.

And she looked down at the hand she was holding. Then, very carefully, she took Nanai's index finger and pushed it into a little triangle.

And she nibbled it.

And then she nibbled it again.

And Nanai's eyes opened.

There was silence. Thu moved back a little as Nanai blinked, her chest filling, her mouth opening in shock. Her hands curled into fists, which she pressed to her cheeks, her arms beginning to shake. And then she moved her hands forward and held them out. She held them out and they hung in the air until Thu took them. And then the two of them were holding each other, rocking in each other's arms, like they were on a ship, both of them crying, Veronique's dad just staring. Finally, they broke apart.

'What's happening?' said Mr Chang.

'It was the café,' Nanai replied. 'When you took me.'

'Café Hoa?'

'Yes.' Nanai didn't take her eyes off Thu. 'And I saw *you*. I thought you were dead. I thought I saw you drown. But you were on the wall. You were in a crowd on another boat.'

'And you hired the tall man, the private investigator,' said Thu.

'But he couldn't find you. Not for ages. I thought I might be wrong, that I was imagining it. But then he DID find you.'

'And now I've found *you*!' Thu added, turning to Veronique's dad, and she pulled him towards her and then the three of them were in each other's arms, so tightly bound that they looked like one person, no questions from any of *us* able to part them. But I still had questions, lots of them, the main ones being: why did Nanai stop eating after Daisy's dad found Thu, and what did the photo of Veronique mean, with the writing on it? I still didn't understand.

So the rest of us sat back and watched, both with them and not with them at the same time, until the nurse spoke again. She still wanted to know what was happening and who we were, so Mrs Chang went through it.

'Wow!' the nurse said. 'That's *wonderful*! But I'll fetch you some towels. You're soaking!'

She was right – the rain had run down my face and down my neck, and Veronique's hair was even shinier than normal.

'Good job you don't have a roof like our school's,' Veronique said, after the nurse had brought the towels.

Mum turned to her. 'What's wrong with it?'

'It's got massive holes in,' I said. 'Half the tiles are missing. Didn't you see? From the helicopter?'

Mum frowned. 'I had my eyes shut. You know how scared I get.'

'And I was busy listening to you,' said Veronique's mum. 'But did you say *holes*? In the school *roof*?'

I nodded. 'Loads of them. The whole place is like a sieve. It's because the tiles are missing.'

'Tiles?' Veronique spun round to me. 'Did you say TILES?'

'Yes. But what about them?'

'Well, there were tiles in Billy's garden,' she said, '*weren't* there? A whole pile of them.'

She was right.

'And there were men,' Mum said. 'Don't you remember when I came to pick you up, Cym? There were men on the school roof!'

'But weren't they up there trying to fix it?'

'How can they have been, if there are *still* so many holes?'

'I . . . don't know.'

And I didn't.

'Well, I wonder why Mrs Martin hasn't done anything about it with the Friends' Forum,' Mum said.

And I stopped. Because I felt like Nanai – like I'd seen a ghost. For a second I thought I was *looking* at Mrs Martin. A nurse further down the ward was chatting to some of the other old people, her laugh warm, her smile wide – and gappy. It wasn't Mrs Martin, though – it was her sister, and seeing her was like being punched again.

Because it was all so obvious.

Mrs Martin *would* have done something about it. That was the whole point. She would NEVER have let our school get so dilapidated. She'd have kicked up fuss after fuss, would have got the parents to write letters to the council and protest – IF she was around. But Mrs Martin WASN'T around. And she wasn't around because someone was being so horrible to her. That person wasn't me. And it *definitely* wasn't Veronique.

I shook my head, but stopped *again*. Because I was suddenly back in Mr Baker's office, as he was making a call.

'Mum,' I said. 'I need your phone. PLEASE.'

And I called a number I knew off by heart, from the

354

time when that person and I *were* friends.

'Billy,' I hissed.

'Oh, Cym,' he whispered. 'You HAVE to come.'

'Wait. *Billy* –' I took a breath – 'you *have* to be honest. DID you do those things to Mrs Martin?'

'No!'

'Really?'

'I SWEAR.'

'But –' I took a breath – 'you know who DID, don't you?'

'Yes,' Billy said. 'And I'm SO sorry. I wanted to say, I really did. But it's going to be too late. You have to COME.'

'Where?'

'You *know* where.'

'Billy!'

'To *school*,' Billy said. 'The meeting's about to start, Cym!'

And in my mind, I saw the letter that Mum had shrugged at, before chucking it on her bedside table.

'Cym? What is it love? What's going on?' she said. She grabbed hold of my wrists and stared at me. Veronique was staring too and so were her mum and dad. Even Jacky Chapman was staring at me and

I stared back, though I couldn't really see him. All I could see were the plans, spread out on Mr Baker's desk.

'They're going to knock our school down,' I said.

CHAPTER FIFTY

This time we really couldn't take the helicopter. It was getting dark and there was no way Jacky Chapman would be allowed to land on the heath. It had taken him ages to get permission in the first place, which is why he hadn't replied to my letter. So as we rushed out the door, Mum got on her phone, and we only had to wait five minutes for the car. Mr Uber again – though neither of the first two.

That is a BIG family.

We'd left Mr Chang and Thu at Nanai's bedside (and Jacky Chapman had gone to move his helicopter off the hospital roof). On the way to school, Mum and Veronique's mum got FURIOUS about Mr Baker's letter.

'I didn't read it properly!' Mum hissed. 'It was all vague for one thing. And I was preoccupied.'

'I was away,' growled Veronique's mum. 'And what with Nanai being ill . . .'

'It doesn't matter,' I said. 'We just have to get there!'

Mr Uber III sped up, then dropped us at the top of the steps. We piled down and ran up to the school gates. The main ones were shut so we pushed open the side entrance and sprinted up to the door. Lights were streaming out of the hall windows. We stopped and looked in – at Mr Baker. He was on the stage, lines of water falling into drip buckets on either side of him. In front of him was a hall full of parents, all looking behind Mr Baker at a screen. On it was a clean, bright digital drawing – of a big shiny building with a sign outside:

ST SAVIOUR'S PRIMARY ACADEMY
BURNHAM LANE

And Billy Lee's dad was standing next to the screen. Grinning.

'Burnham Lane?' Mum shouted. 'That's MILES away. It's nowhere NEAR here!'

'Come on!' I said.

But this time we really were too late.

We barrelled through the main door and into the corridor where the trophy cabinet is. We spun round, past the Year 1 coat pegs and up to the hall door. But we stopped. In front of us were two MASSIVE men, both in high-vis vests. The door behind them was open but they stood in our way. The nearest one folded his arms across his chest.

'Sorry. Meeting's about to finish. No more entry.'

'Let us in!' Mum demanded. But the two men moved together like a wall.

'Can't. Not once official proceedings have begun.'

'Nonsense!' Mum tried to barge past, but one of the men blocked her.

'Let us through!' Veronique demanded, but both men shook their heads.

I peered through their legs – at Mr Baker.

'So,' he was saying, 'and to conclude: the current school buildings are *too* old and no longer viable. It would cost a fortune to make them right again and they'd still be too small for a growing school community. The new building will not only be perfect, but will be built to our needs by a reputable local company. And *this* site here will provide valuable new housing for local residents! So, all in favour, raise your hands and we can look forward to a bright new future!'

And the parents looked up at him as they thought about it. They chatted among themselves. A few at the front didn't look sure, one couple arguing. But most were nodding! And they were about to raise their hands. Mum rushed to get in, but one of the men held her back. The other stepped forward to block Veronique's mum – but they couldn't stop *me*.

I didn't rush in, though. Who'd listen to a kid? Instead I dug my hands in my pockets. I pulled out the contents and flung them through the guard's legs, the hard, dry peas skittering across the shiny wood floor.

As Veronique let go of Kit-Kat.

And there was MAYHEM!

The two security guards screamed. Mr Baker jumped on to the table and knocked off the laptop while chairs were kicked over in the audience. People at the back fled into the kitchen. The rest scrambled up the wall bars, while Billy's dad waved his arms.

'Calm down!' he cried. 'He's just a pet. He lives next door, lovely little fella. We still have to vote!' he shouted.

And they did. After Veronique had put Kit-Kat back on her shoulder, everyone edged back towards their seats – as Mum ran up on to the stage. And she told them – about everything that had been done to Mrs Martin by Mr Baker so she WOULDN'T BE HERE. So she WOULDN'T OBJECT. She even told them about the blue jelly from Billy's house and I thought that would be it, more than enough to make people see THE TRUTH. But Mr Baker shouted, 'Lies!' and 'Rubbish!' while Billy's dad said it was nonsense.

'Come on!' he said. 'They don't want change, that's all. They don't want *progress*.'

'All those in favour!' demanded Mr Baker.

And the audience was still – until a hand went up. I couldn't believe it, but it did. And another. Then another! I stared, open-mouthed, because who could believe Mr Baker over MY MUM? Quite a few people, it seemed, because two hands went up together and then more as I swallowed and stared, feeling queasy and sick as about half the parents held their hands up. So would we lose it? Our WHOLE school? Like Nanai and Thu had lost their home? Would people really vote so *that* would happen – after Mr Baker had cheated, and wrecked the place, and lied to them?

I'll never know. Because at that moment, someone else stepped forward.

And he walked up to the stage.

'Son?'

But Billy Lee kept going, up to the table where he set down his new Chelsea bag.

'*Son?*' Mr Lee said again, menace in his voice now. But Billy ignored it, and looked out at the audience.

'This was in our garden,' he said, his voice all wobbly. 'There are loads of them.'

And he lifted out a roof tile.

There were gasps. Someone shouted, 'Outrageous!' Then there was silence (except for the drip buckets). It was only broken when the door was thrown open and in strode the best captain ANY TEAM has ever had.

And behind Jacky Chapman were the police.

CHAPTER FIFTY-ONE

The tiles in Billy's garden were from our school roof. His dad's fingerprints were on them. Mr Baker's weren't, but Mrs Martin had kept her mangled sports bag and they were all over that. CCTV from the Sutcliffe Park athletics club car park also showed Mr Baker spraying her car, while we had all been distracted by Billy and his 'sore' stomach. Mum told us about it – in Veronique's living room the next day. We all said, 'Wow!' and 'How could he?' and then Mum told us they'd also found out that Mr Baker owned half of Billy's dad's building company.

'They'd have made millions,' she said.

'But it's all okay now?'

Mum said yes. And she was about to tell us more,

but Veronique's dad came in with a cup of tea.

For Thu.

Thu was staying with them. I'd been desperate to see her again – ever since leaving her at the hospital with Nanai. Mum had said no to going round first thing. It was a very difficult time, we had to give the family space. It was SO frustrating! But now it was late afternoon and I was studying Thu as we sat in the living room, her eyes SO very much like Veronique's, and I hoped I could finally put together the last pieces of the puzzle.

'Thu,' I said, after she'd had a sip of tea, 'will you tell us what happened to you, please? And to Nanai?'

I *needed* to know. There was still a big part of the story that wasn't there.

Thu took a breath, then glanced at the one empty chair in the room. And then she stared – looking a bit fierce, like Nanai used to be with me. I thought she might refuse, or ask what I meant. But she knew exactly what I wanted to know and after a second she gave a nod.

And we all listened.

'They smashed our windows,' Thu said, her voice very deliberate, and slow.

I nodded. 'Back home?'

Thu's eyes flashed. 'Brighton is my home.'

'I know. Sorry, I meant before. In . . . Vietnam?'

'Yes.' Thu blinked. 'It was the first thing. We thought it must be hooligans. But it wasn't. It was people we knew, people we thought were our friends. Our neighbours. Normal people.'

'And then?'

'This is very hard for me, Cymbeline. I have never told anyone this.'

'But you should tell your story, shouldn't you? So people know.'

'Yes. That's true. So I will try. So –' Thu took a massive breath – 'they set fire to our house.'

'*What?* The same people?'

'When we were sleeping. Can you believe it? We managed to put it out but they went to the factory that our father owned.'

'And burned that?'

'Yes.'

'What did you do?'

'Us? Nothing. But our father went to the police.'

'And did they help him?'

'No. We . . .'

'Yes?'

Thu turned towards me but her mind was somewhere else. 'We never saw him again,' she said.

'Oh. So . . . you decided to leave?'

'No.' Thu paused. 'I couldn't even swim. And we were scared. And there was another reason. But then . . .'

'Yes?'

'They killed my husband,' she said, 'in broad daylight. Just . . . killed him. With sticks. And they were going to kill us too. They even started to hit us. But Nanai knew one of them. Even though they had masks on, she knew him. And she called out his name, begging for our lives. So they let us go. And we ran to the docks. We gave all our money to some men and climbed on to a fishing boat.'

'Was it terrible?'

'No – because we were safe. Or thought we were. We sang songs, we shared our food. But . . .'

Thu stopped and her lips trembled, so much fear in her eyes that I knew what she was going to tell us. I'd seen it, in Café Hoa. But now Thu made it real, describing the waves and the darkness, people screaming as they were swept overboard right in front of her eyes. Old people. Children. She and Nanai clung to the mast, and to each other.

'Until this huge wave tore us apart. For a second we stared at each other. But then I was flung up into the air, and then down into the water, up and down, the water like a thousand punches, until it sucked me right down. But I didn't die. So many did, so why not me? Just as I was losing consciousness, the sea spat me out. And there was another fishing boat, arms reaching to pull me in, though I fought them.'

'You . . . ?'

'Fought them. Because I didn't *want* to be rescued. My father and my husband . . . And now my sister. My *twin* sister. I wanted to stay in the sea, but they wouldn't let me drown. And then the storm died and a bigger boat came and took us all.'

'To Hong Kong?'

'No. To Singapore. I just stood on deck and stared at the sea, at all the broken pieces, the suitcases and the baskets. And the people.'

'And then you came to live here?'

'Eventually, yes.'

'And you thought Nanai was dead?' asked Veronique.

Thu nodded at that, looking very small and alone on the sofa. And I could understand it. The terrible storm, the miracle that she herself had survived. 'I lived my life,' Thu said. 'And . . .'

'Yes?'

'I let Nanai became a memory.'

'Until Daisy's dad came?'

Thu nodded again, as Mr Chang let out a long, slow breath. He stood up and joined her on the sofa, his arms going round her, while Veronique grabbed hold of her hand. Mum just bit her lip, tears rolling down her face, until Mrs Chang passed her a tissue. But I didn't cry, and I didn't go to comfort her.

Because it still did NOT make sense.

'No.'

My voice was louder than I'd meant it to be. Everyone turned.

'Cym?' Mum said. 'Please don't talk like that. Thu's just told us something *really* difficult.'

'But not all of it,' I said.

'What do you mean?'

I turned to Thu. For a second I nearly just forgot it, but we had to know the truth.

The WHOLE truth.

'You sent the photo *back*,' I said.

Mum frowned. 'The . . . ?'

'*Photo*. Of *Veronique*. Nanai sent it with Daisy's dad, when he went to Sea View Care Home. It had "Granddaughter" written on the back.' I turned again to Thu. 'You sent it back, and you told Daisy's dad you didn't want to see Nanai, didn't you?'

Slowly, Thu nodded.

'But why? *Why* did you? It's what made her ill. It's why she stopped eating – because you didn't want to see her after she'd found you. You have to tell us *why*.'

'I didn't want to upset you,' Thu said, though she didn't mean me: she'd turned to glance at Veronique before staring at her dad.

'*Me?*' he said.

Thu nodded. 'You have a life. You have a family and a daughter.'

Mr Chang laughed. 'So? How could it upset me to know that you're alive? When I've thought all my life you were dead? How could it upset me to have an amazing new auntie?'

'Because she's not your auntie,' Nanai said.

Nanai was standing in the doorway. She'd been asleep when we'd arrived, down in her cabin. And then they did tell us the truth, both of them together, the very last piece of it. Like a long but simple word, emerging out of a jumble of Scrabble letters.

CHAPTER FIFTY-TWO

Thu had had a baby. It was born six months before they fled. That was the first thing they told us (after Nanai had sat down next to Thu). It made me swallow, because I remembered the photo that I'd seen – the parcel, all wrapped up, next to the screaming woman. For a second I wondered if Veronique and I should hear what happened next – weren't we too young? But if these things happen to kids younger than us, how could it be wrong for us to know them? Anyway, I didn't get a choice because Thu went on. And she described the storm again, though this time including her baby. How it had screamed, how she'd clung on to it, how Nanai had clung on to both of them.

'Until we began to fight,' said Nanai, glancing at Thu.

'To . . .' None of us thought we'd heard right. Veronique's dad stared at her.

'Yes. *Fight*.'

'But . . . why?'

'She was screaming,' said Thu. 'Not the baby. Nanai. Screaming! At first I didn't understand. I couldn't hear her. It was too loud. The waves. The roar. But then I realised she wasn't just screaming like the others, she was screaming at *me*. Into my face. 'You can't swim!' she yelled. 'You can't SWIM!' Over and over as the boat lurched, until finally she did it.'

'She . . . ?'

'She pulled my baby out of my arms.' And Thu turned to Veronique's dad once again. And said, '*You*.'

'What?'

'You. She took *you*. And I went under. And down.'

Nanai was crying now. 'I'm so sorry,' she said. 'I've always been so sorry.'

'No,' said Thu, grabbing hold of Nanai's hand. 'You were right, I couldn't swim, the baby would have died.' She turned to Veronique's dad. 'You would have died, you were so small. But I wept and wept for you, all my life. I was like a Russian doll without the centre. Because I thought Nanai was gone and *you* were gone, until the tall man came to see me. And I was *so* happy. I was, really.'

'Then why did you send him away?' Mr Chang asked.

Thu squeezed Nanai's hand tighter. '*Because!* What if I came back? It would upset things. I knew that Nanai loved you. The tall man told me all about your life. I knew that Nanai had been your mother all this time. She saved you. But then . . .'

'You saw me,' said Veronique.

And Thu nodded. 'I saw you. In the flesh. You suddenly appeared. Not just a picture. Like a miracle. My granddaughter. And you told me my sister was ill. And so I'm here.'

And so she was, which is about the end of this story. But not quite. Veronique's dad was stunned. But then he hugged Thu again. And then he hugged Nanai. And everyone hugged – me joining in this time. Mr Chang kept calling Thu 'Mother', Thu called him 'Son'. They shook with tears, and laughter, and I shook too, until Mum drew me away.

'This is their time now,' she said.

And she was right. I'd known there was more to the story, more to the mystery.

But now it was time for us to go. They didn't even notice us leave.

CHAPTER FIFTY-THREE

So we left them there, in the living room together, though I still had so many questions.

'But why didn't Nanai ever tell him?' I asked.

Mum shrugged. 'Maybe it was easier. She didn't want to burden him with knowing. She was going to be his mother, so why let him think anything else? And it would have made it so much easier to be accepted in this country and to stay here.'

Veronique said the same thing, next day outside school. It's what they'd all guessed after Mum and I'd left.

'He might have spent his whole life pining for his real mum,' Veronique said. 'And I might always have wanted my real grandma.'

'And maybe Nanai felt guilty,' I said. 'She did the right thing, but it must also have been really hard for her.'

Veronique nodded. 'At least we all get to be together now,' she said.

And then we both walked in through the gates, where we got pats on the back and thumbs up from the teachers and all the parents, people wanting to know how we'd worked it all out about Mr Baker and Billy's dad, and their scheme for the new building. One person was more grateful than all the rest of them put together.

Mrs Martin.

She was there that morning. Back where she belonged. She remembered our special greetings from Year 3 and then gave us a massive hug.

'Don't thank us, though,' I said, after she'd let us go. 'Daisy helped, and so did Lance and Vi. But you really have to thank *him*,' I said, pointing to the gates. 'He was the REALLY brave one.'

And so Mrs Martin ran over and gave Billy Lee the biggest hug EVER.

After school on Friday, Billy came back to our house

and we played Subbuteo, though at half time I had a thought and ran downstairs.

'But, Mum,' I said.

'Yes, Cym?'

'It's movie night.'

'Ah.'

'Aren't you going?'

Mum sighed. 'Not . . . tonight, Cym.'

'Why not? Aren't you supposed to be seeing loads more of Stephan?'

'No,' Mum said.

'*No?* But why not?'

'Well, I decided that, in the end, I don't want to see loads more of him.'

'Don't you? Why?'

'I don't know. That perfume he bought me . . . maybe you were right. It didn't smell like me.'

'What do you mean?'

'I dunno. It's hard, what with everything. You . . . Stephan's girls.'

'But they're great!' I said. 'Specially the little one. Aren't we going to see them any more?'

'*What?*'

'And Stephan's great too. I thought he was going to

be round here loads. All the time maybe!'

'He was! We were hoping to . . . But it didn't seem like you wanted that!'

'*Me?* Nonsense. Are you seriously saying that you've told him you're not going to see him any more?'

Mum didn't answer that. She just stared at me in complete disbelief for some reason. 'Oh, Cymbeline!' she said.

And went to find her phone.

I went back upstairs to Billy and we finished our game.

Charlton 7–6 Chelsea.

YES!

Jacky Chapman (miniature version) got the winner.

CHAPTER FIFTY-FOUR

And that's it, the end – or it would be if *I* could choose. In fact, I'd give anything for that to be the end – but stories aren't like that. They have their own endings, which you have to accept, no matter how much you wish you didn't. And this story goes right back to the beginning.

Billy and I finished our game and had supper, then his mum came to pick him up. Over a cup of tea she told Mum that she'd had no idea what her *idiot husband* had been up to. She also said that the police weren't going to arrest him – not now he'd put all the tiles back on our school roof. There was a possibility that the local authority might have wanted the police to press charges for fraud, but they just wanted to *sweep it all under the carpet*, as Billy's mum put it. 'They don't need the attention.'

As for Mr Baker, he'd vanished.

'With all the cash from the business account,' Mrs Lee said. 'Looks like we're going to have to cut back a bit. Not a bad thing, if you ask me. It's friends that make you happy, isn't it, Billy love? Not *stuff*.'

Billy nodded, and his mum took him home.

We had football practice in the morning (no helicopters) and afterwards I went round to Veronique's. She got her Grade 5 result – just a pass because she'd only played two pieces and she hadn't done her sight reading – and then we went down to the little wooden house at the bottom of their garden. Where Nanai used to live.

Which is where you joined the story, right back at the start.

It was quiet in there. And dusty. Cold. We stood for a minute, looking down at Nanai's chair. It was even emptier than the rest of the place. There was a hollowed-out bit, like the empty spaces we'd seen at the Pompeii exhibition at the British Museum.

And seeing it made Veronique cry.

Until her dad came in. He said not to mind about her Grade 5 and she laughed, amazed he'd think that that's why she was upset. Then she looked at him.

'Will she ever come back?'

Mr Chang smiled. 'I hope so. But we have to let her do what she wants. They've a great deal of catching up to do, you know.'

He meant Thu – and Nanai, who'd left together a few days after they'd finally told us their story.

'Where are they now?' I said.

Veronique's dad told us they were in Hanoi, staying in a hotel, before they went back to the town they grew up in. They hadn't set a date to return home here, so I could understand why Veronique had asked whether they'd ever come back, but to picture Nanai out there was amazing, especially as she'd nearly died. But Thu had brought her back to life. She'd started eating only minutes after we'd dashed off from the hospital to get to the meeting at school. The next day she was back at home again – and playing football a few days after that.

'Thu's hopeless, though,' Nanai whispered to me, the last time I saw her before they left for Vietnam. 'No ball control. Just closes her eyes and boots it!

She's going to have to play for Mil—'

'*Shhhhh!*' I said.

'Sorry. The Team Who Shall Not Be Named!'

And now the two of them were in Vietnam, having fun together, being sisters again, in the places where they grew up.

Which, I imagine, leaves you wondering why Veronique was crying.

Well.

Here goes.

Deep breath.

Mr Chang sighed. 'Come on, then. It's time. We can't put it off any longer.'

And we followed him outside, and further down their garden, where Mum and Mrs Chang, and even Auntie Mill and Juni and Uncle Chris were waiting.

In a little circle.

Because rats don't live that long, you see. And Kit-Kat was already quite old when Veronique's dad brought him home from his lab. And that morning Veronique had woken up to find her room quiet, no twitching in the corner, no little face looking out through his bars.

And now it was time to say goodbye to him.

He'd been epic, though. I tried to tell Veronique that, though she was crying so much she couldn't hear me. She couldn't hold the that box her dad handed her either, so I helped her with it, both of us kneeling down to the small hole that Mr Chang had dug. And, very gently, we laid Kit-Kat into it, Veronique sprinkling peas beside him, her mum a bit of croissant. I put in my favourite Subbuteo ball, and then Veronique's dad spoke of how he'd seen Kit-Kat at work and immediately known he was special. Her mum spoke about how gentle he was, my mum smiling as she remembered how she'd thought he was a hamster. (She only realised what he really was when he'd gone and saved our school.) Veronique just whispered that she loved him. And it was my turn.

'The Jacky Chapman of rats,' I said.

And then Veronique's dad covered him in a blanket of earth.

The adults and Juni left then, to go next door. Veronique and I stayed there alone a while, until her tears dried up, both of us smiling when we thought of Kit-Kat. The wonder of him. How keen he always was: to play, to learn, to eat and drink, and just to BE – in this wonderful thing called life.

And then it was time for us to go too. So we patted down the soil on top of Kit-Kat and turned, Veronique's hand in mine as she led me over to the side of their garden, then through the hole in the fence – to Auntie Mill's.

It was brilliant then.

It was still only February but Uncle Chris had got the barbecue out, him and Veronique's dad and my cousin Clay huffing and puffing round it while Mum and Auntie Mill and Veronique's mum laughed at them. We kids all poured drinks, sorted chairs and set the table (EVEN Juni helped).

Then, while the flames on the barbecue died down, we all talked about what had happened. One thing that stood out for me was how Veronique had taken the blame for the writing on Mrs Martin's car. She'd done it for me. It made me glow inside to think she'd do that. It made me feel really connected to her. Maybe when we were grown-ups we'd remember it, like Nanai remembered the nibble on her finger which Thu used to wake her up.

'It was their thing,' Veronique said, 'which

they've always done, ever since they were small.'

'And Nanai's done to *you*, all *your* life.'

'I know,' said Veronique, and I could tell she wished Nanai was there to do it now. I smiled. But then I frowned, and asked her what it was like to know that Nanai wasn't her real granny after all.

'But she is,' Veronique said. 'Words can't change that. I've got both of them now, that's all.' She turned to her dad. 'And so do you.'

'And so do I,' said Mr Chang. 'You're right, Veronique. It's not what words you use. It's how you feel, right?'

Veronique nodded and then there was a knock on the side gate and we all turned as Stephan came through to the garden, his littlest girl nearly knocking me over when she charged up to me. Mum ran over to Stephan and he kissed her and hugged her, and then she told us all to shush. There was something she needed to show us. So we all did shush and watched as she took the little box out of her bag – the one I'd seen the night the dhal went flying.

I stepped forward, but it wasn't for me, actually. And I did not care ONE bit.

Mum took out a diamond ring, which sparkled in the light from the window as she slid it down on to her finger.

'Since I never answered properly . . .' she said to Stephan, turning to look at him. 'The answer is . . .'

'YES!' I shouted.

And Mum beamed at me, then beamed at Stephan, and Stephan beamed at everyone.

Mum had brought something called halloumi for Stephan to have. She dropped slices of it on to the barbecue – next to the thirty-five-day matured grass-fed Irish rib-eye.

THANKS, Uncle Chris!

And then we all sat down to eat. And I mean *all* of us, because Veronique's dad had a surprise. He borrowed Auntie Mill and Uncle Chris's mended iPad and soon there they were, Nanai and Thu, on a pile of magazines, waving to us all from Vietnam.

'Hi, Mums,' Mr Chang said, waving back.

'Hi, Nanais,' Veronique said, waving too.

It was fabulous. So fabulous in fact that even Juni was happy. After FINALLY noticing my haircut (remember?) and telling me it looked rubbish, she turned to her dad.

'Perfectly *à point*,' she said.

And I agreed. That steak – it was almost as good as pizza. Though the best thing was simply that we were all, just, well, sort of, *there*.

Together.

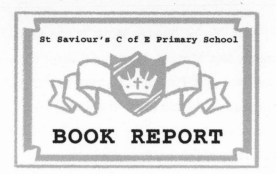

St Saviour's C of E Primary School

BOOK REPORT

Name: Cymbeline Igloo

Teacher: Miss Phillips

Name of Book: WAR AND PEACE

Author: Leo Tolstoy

Rating: NO stars

Review: This book is one hundred per cent RUBBISH. You so should not waste your time on this book. There is probably a film of it. Most of it is Peace, and the War doesn't come for ages. I mean AGES. I'm surprised the soldiers could still remember how to fire their rifles. Or that they didn't just die of boredom. There are about three hundred pages of Peace. Calling it WAR AND PEACE is a con because you expect the War FIRST. It should be called 'Peace and War'.

Or 'Peace, Peace, Peace, More Peace and War (Though Not Much)'. You could skip straight to the War but I wouldn't even bother doing that because it isn't even that good. There are no pictures. And after the French FINALLY do attack the Russians, guess what?

It's a draw.

A DRAW!!

All that and it's 0–0! And you don't know who anyone is because they've all got six names each. Jacky Chapman would be Jacky Chapmanov (I think) or Ivan Chapmanov or Vanya Chapmanov or Ivan Ivanovich, or Jacky Jackovich Chapmanovich, by which time you'd have completely forgotten who he was. Or which side he was on. And then, in the end, when the French actually DO win – guess what?

They just go home!

So why did they bother coming in the first place?

Honestly! WAR AND PEACE is totally terrible, the only good thing being the bits where you learn what war does to the normal people whose houses are all destroyed and have to flee. It made me think of Nanai and Thu.

So maybe it's not THAT bad.

Should we order copies of this book for the school library?
NO.
Would you recommend this book to a friend?
YES (as a joke).
Which character did you most identify with?
The Tsar. He wasn't in it much but he kept telling the others to get on with the fighting.
Would you read another book by the same author?
HE WROTE OTHER BOOKS?! NOOOOOOO!!!!!! Why did they let him?!
Which part of the book did you most enjoy?
The end.

ACKNOWLEDGEMENTS

So many people helped me write this book, some in ways they'll never know. Nghiem Ta gave me great advice about the experience of refugees from Vietnam. Naomi Delap offered support and ideas, while Dan and Helen Delap let me live in their house while I was writing it. Franklin Baron, Viola Baron and Frieda Baron pushed me through to the end. Benji Davies's wonderful illustrations once more help to bring Cymbeline and his friends to life. Nick Lake's insights during the editing process were fabulous, as was the support of the rest of the HarperCollins team, including Jo-Anna Parkinson, Jessica Dean, Samantha Stewart, Jessica Williams and Sarah Hall. Cathryn Summerhayes at Curtis Brown continues to be agent supreme. Mostly, however, I'd like to thank the thousands of teachers, librarians and young people who have embraced Cymbeline by reading about him, writing to me, welcoming me to their schools or dressing up as him on World Book Day.